Storm
Chaser

Cheryl Weavers Stacey

Storm Chaser
Cheryl Weavers Stacey

This book is a work of fiction. Names, characters, places, and incidents are the product of the author's imagination or are used fictitiously. Any resemblance to actual events, locales, or persons living or dead is coincidental.

Storm Chaser

Introduction

In 1964, cell phones, credit cards, personal computers, and microwaves awaited discovery. Men in white uniforms delivered milk in glass bottles to neighborhood doors. In the city, giant department stores offered consumer goods, while shoppers browsed stores in suburban shopping centers. Paper bags, rather than plastic ones, held their purchased goods.

Girls wore dresses or skirts and blouses or sweaters, and Penny loafers, Mary James or saddle shoes to school. Curled hair was teased into what some called "rats nests." Boys wore button down shirts, dress pants, belts, and nice socks and dress shoes. A substantial amount of hair product held boys hair in place. Jeans and t-shirts were scarce. Gym required uniforms and gym shoes. Tennis shoes were worn on the tennis court.

Most students succeeded in school. Failure was attributed to laziness. A trip to the dean's office and his paddle corrected most attitude and behavior issues. Students grouped in cliques: jocks, cheerleaders and pep squad, hoods (bad boys and girls), and the rest of us who went through the day pretty much anonymous. Though marijuana use was on the rise, most young people got in trouble for smoking cigarettes, drinking beer, and having sex. Few students dropped out. The girls who did were pregnant. Some boys dropped out to go to work.

Entertainment revolved around pop music blaring from transistor radios and 45 records. Hollywood catered to youth with beach movies. Downtown theatres had balconies and drive-in theatres dotted suburbia. School dances followed Friday night football games. Adults dressed up and danced to bands in nightclubs.

Dining ran the gamut from fancy restaurants, cafeterias, lunch counters, diners, to the fast food at McDonalds or Burger King. A new food fad was pizza sold by the slice in Pizza Parlors.

Families went to church together. Ladies and girls wore hats and gloves. Men and boys wore suits. Catholic masses were in Latin. Protestant choirs proclaimed anthems as congregations sang hymns and choruses. Revival meetings were well attended, often lasting weeks. Some were held in tents and crossed denominational lines. Women served in churches as teachers and in women's social or missionary auxiliary groups. All important church leaders were men.

Most women, especially those with young children, didn't work. Because few daycares were available, family and neighbors provided childcare. Jobs were plentiful for those wanting to work. Office skills taught in high school prepared young women for secretarial jobs and telephone operators. Beauty schools attracted some girls and so did working as a waitress. Some girls pursued education for a nursing career or teaching. Graduating boys passing up college joined the military or joined skill trades such as mechanics & electronics.

A girl often married shortly after high school or during college, moving from her parent's home to her husband's. Once married, a couple lived within what they made. Major purchases were charged to revolving accounts. There were the rich, middle class, and poor. Some got help from time to time but nobody lived on welfare. That would soon change with the legislation associated with "The Great Society" enacted in 1964.

A change in American culture came about by those promoting women's liberation, a philosophy that told women they weren't worth anything if they didn't get a paycheck. When these women began going into the workplace, homes became fractured and children grew confused about family roles. Often new relationships developed for these women, leaving broken homes in their wake. Divorce statistics began to climb.

The November 1963 assassination of President John F. Kennedy continued to be investigated and debated. His successor, Lyndon B. Johnson, pushed the Civil Rights Act legislation and congress passed it in 1964. The promise looked good on paper but was a hard sale to predominantly white America. Public schools began the slow process of integration and private schools flourished as white Americans resisted the change of culture.

In world politics, America was pitted against communism promoted by Russia. The current battleground, Viet Nam in southeast Asia continued as a high school debate topic and cause of concern for boys turning eighteen and required to register for the draft. An unpopular war from the beginning, the Viet Nam conflict would fracture the American public viciously before the end of the decade.

This was America in 1964 when Penny Wilburn was sixteen. This is her story.

Dedication

This book is dedicated to my daughter, Laura who

- amazes me with her indomitable spirit and strength of character,
- pursues the best of life and makes everything around her beautiful,
- is an awesome wife, mother, friend, and
- above all, is a beautiful daughter who I love very much.

1

Penny Wilburn crouched under her bed covers while flashes of lightning and thunder reverberated through the room like punches of a boxing champion. Her childhood dread of storms had dissipated some through the years as she gained a greater understanding of weather systems but she never totally relaxed during a storm. She had lost too much to the ravages of violent weather.

When Penny was seven years old, a severe thunderstorm produced a tornado that tore a path through the North Carolina farming community where she lived. Forty seven people died, including Penny's parents, grandparents, and dear Aunt Helen. She had been living with her aunt and uncle while her parents traveled with a carnival, returning from a three-month circuit in Florida for a week at Easter when the tornado struck, destroying the row of homes where her entire family lived.

Penny's fingers rubbed the satin binding of the quilt Aunt Helen had made from Penny's outgrown dresses. The quilt and the nightgown she wore was all she was left with that night. Uncle Bear, as she called him, had grabbed her up from her bed and carried her to the storm shelter. Aunt Helen was behind them. A few feet from the shelter door a falling tree struck and killed her just as Penny and her uncle whirled around to make sure she was coming. Pulling the door to and latching it securely, Baron Sanford huddled with Penny in a corner of the shelter until the storm's fury subsided. When they came out, they found Helen's body crumbled under the large branch of an oak tree that still had the ropes from Penny's swing. Gone was the Sanford house as were the houses where Penny's grandparents and parents lived and died, their bodies lying among the debris scattered over a two mile stretch of countryside.

A soft knocking at the door drew Penny from the cocoon she had wrapped herself in. Her bare feet scampered across the cold wooden floor to the door. Accustomed to roommates, she answered the knocking with a whisper.

"Who is it?"

"Penny, it's me."

Penny recognized the voice of Mrs. Gibson, the dorm mother at Mason Hall, the dormitory where Penny lived as a freshman and sophomore. The first five years at Charlotte Hills, Penny lived with her uncle in their apartment. When she started the high school program, Baron was told anonymous funds had been given to cover Penny's dormitory fees. Believing this would help Penny's socialization, he agreed and Penny began to live in a room with three other girls. The other girls at Mason Hall had mothers who wrote letters, called on birthdays, and welcomed them home on holidays. But Penny didn't and Mrs. Gibson had always made sure Penny felt loved and secure. Knowing the young girl's background, the dorm mother checked on Penny during storms.

Penny opened the door.

"Hi, Penny. May I come in? It's cold in this drafty old hall."

"Of course, come in Mrs. Gibson. What are you doing here at Bryant?"

Rebecca Gibson stepped across the threshold, her eyes quickly perusing the dorm room occupied by the high school junior. The space, furnished with a bed, dresser, and desk for each of the two girls who would share the room, was spacious and pleasant. Dark molding lined the floor, ceiling, window and door frames, a striking contrast to the tint of white paint on the walls. The one window, framed with bleached muslin panels, was directly across the room from the door, dividing the room into the two parts to be occupied by each girl. She turned her attention to Penny.

"Dean Merrick reassigned me to Bryant Hall for the new term. You don't mind, do you?" She grinned.

"How wonderful! I so hated leaving you behind at Mason. I've missed you this summer. Did you have a good time?"

"I did. Being on the summer staff at Ridgecrest was wonderful but I'm glad to be back. The school moved my furnishings last week and I'll be spending today unpacking."

The two sat on Penny's bed and chatted as the early morning thunderstorm faded. They talked about the new dorm and how different living with one girl would be from the group of four girls who shared a room previously.

"Penny, just think. Instead of three roommates, you have just one. Should be a lot quieter for studying."

"That's going to be a plus. I was hoping maybe Julia or one of the other girls I've been roommates with would share my room this year."

"I know. Are you o.k. with rooming with someone new?"

"I guess. Sure. My old friends are still here. A girl can't have too many friends can she?

"No, she can't. Your new roommate will be blessed to know you."

"Can you tell me anything about her?"

"I know this is her first boarding school experience. Her father is a United States Senator. Courtney has excellent grades and has registered for advanced classes like you. That's probably why you were paired as roommates."

"When's she coming?"

"Later today. I'm glad you got settled in here first. Your bed is moved away from the window. Did you do that?"

"Well, you know—storms and all. Uncle Bear helped me carry my stuff here and swapped the bed and desk. I like it better by the window. See that tree branch? I'll be able to watch the birds and squirrels while I study. And when it's stormy, well, I'll be across the room away from it."

"Good idea. Did the storm wake you this morning?"

"Yes, ma'am. It was pretty strong for awhile. Glad it's passed."

"Me, too."

#####

Penny never doubted Mrs. Gibson cared about her. A few weeks after she came to Charlotte Hills, Penny ran to a closet during a thunderstorm. Mrs. Gibson coaxed her out and sat on the floor holding her until the storm passed, softly singing hymns Penny recognized from the little church she had gone to with Aunt Helen.

"Mrs. Gibson, do you know about church?"

"Yes, Penny. I know about church. That's where I learned these songs. Did you like to go to church?"

"Oh, yes!" Penny replied as she closed her eyes and drifted into a peaceful sleep.

Mrs. Gibson took up the torch of Penny's spiritual training. She got permission from Baron Sanford for Penny to ride the bus that carried students to a local Baptist church for Sunday School and worship. Penny looked forward to the trip off campus for church that she enjoyed so much.

#####

"I hope she is a Christian and will go to church with me." Penny turned the conversation back to the unknown roommate.

Rebecca Gibson smiled at the fervor of Penny's Christian faith, so similar to her own at that age. Abandoned as a baby and reared in a Baptist orphanage, Rebecca established an early relationship with the Lord that grew expeditiously during her childhood. She also learned from loving house parents you didn't need to be blood kin to be family. Earning a full scholarship to college, Rebecca graduated with honors from the University of North Carolina and became a social worker. After several years working for the state of North Carolina, she married Robb Gibson, a successful real estate broker. A year later, just as the couple decided to start a family, Robb was killed in a airplane crash. Suddenly alone, twenty-five-year-old Rebecca sold the brokerage business and was looking for opportunities in social work when she came across the job as a dorm mother at Charlotte Hills Academy, a girls' preparatory boarding school west of Charlotte. The position gave Rebecca the combination of work and ministry she wanted and the opportunity to be a mom, a dream she felt had died with her husband. For ten years, she loved all the girls at Charlotte Hills but had found a special place in her heart for Penny.

"Penny, I don't know if she is a Christian. If she is, it will be wonderful for you to have a sister in the Lord to live with. If she isn't, well, you can invite her to come to church with you, though she no doubt will not be staying on campus over the weekends. But living your faith will be your best witness. Just be yourself. Everybody loves you here and she will, too."

"Yes, ma'am." Penny appreciated Mrs. Gibson's guidance and mentoring. Moving to Bryant Hall was wonderful but leaving Mrs. Gibson behind had been a loss for Penny. God had been so good to take care of that need.

The dorm mother looked at her watch. "Look at the time! The dining room will be open for breakfast in ten minutes. I'll wait for you downstairs while you get dressed then we'll go see if the cooking is as good here at Bryant as it is at Mason."

Penny scurried into a cotton skirt and white blouse and the two went to the dining room to enjoy their first breakfast at Bryant Hall.

2

Penny spent the morning getting her desk and closet organized. She had never been one to have a lot of things and had chosen carefully what clothes she would bring to the dorm, keeping the rest at her uncle's apartment. When everything was neatly placed, she joined some of her friends for lunch then returned to her room and lay down to take a nap.

Suddenly the door burst open and a tall, blond girl stepped into the room. Penny quietly peeked from under her quilt and watched her throw a small overnight case on the bed and walk straight to the window. A woman and older man followed, the man carrying two large suitcases. The man dropped the suitcases and stepped back into the hallway, closing the door behind him.

"Mother, look at this view! All I can see is a barn. You said this place was picturesque!" Courtney whined.

The woman walked to the window and pulled back the curtain.

"Courtney, it's a beautiful campus. And that's the stable where the horses are boarded. Look what a nice room you have."

At that point Penny stirred from under the covers and sat up.

"Oh, hello," the woman said. "I didn't realize someone was in here. We must be in the wrong room."

"No, ma'am. I'm Penny Wilburn, Courtney's roommate."

Courtney stared wide eyed at the petite brunette.

"Roommate! Mother, I thought I was going to have a private room!" she wailed.

"The private rooms are for seniors." Penny slipped off the bed and offered her hand to the newcomer.

"Hi, I'm Penny."

Courtney ignored the gesture and sat down on the other bed. Mrs. Guilford quickly stepped up and accepted Penny's hand.

"It's very nice to meet you, Penny. Have you been at Charlotte Hills very long?"

"Yes, ma'am, eight years. I came after my parents died. I love it here."

"Eight years! You were what, eight years old? Did you hear that Courtney? Penny must really know this place and the people well."

"She doesn't have any choice, does she? You want me to be roommates with little orphan Annie?"

"Courtney!" her mother chided.

Courtney, still ignoring Penny, snatched the latch open on the overnight case and dumped its contents on the bed. She pulled open a drawer of the dresser and complained again.

"Ewe! Rosebuds! Mother, there are rosebud liners in these drawers!"

"That's no problem, dear. We'll go shopping for new liners." Mrs. Guilford turned to Penny. "Do you have the same liners? Maybe we could switch dressers."

"Sorry, all the dressers are the same. The school puts in new liners every summer before the school year begins. Some of the girls change it. You can if you want."

"I want!" Courtney pouted. "Rosebuds, a barn for a view and an orphan for a roommate! I want to change a lot of things!"

Penny felt like an interloper in her own room. Despite the burning in her throat, she smiled weakly and excused herself.

"Ma'am, it was very nice to meet you. I'll leave you two alone to get moved in."

As she went down the steps, she saw the older man struggle to enter the front door with a trunk. Penny held the door open and offered to help him carry the trunk up the stairs.

"No thank you, miss. The steps have carpet. I'll just pull it from here. Appreciate your help and offer, though."

The man nodded and smiled as he backed up the stairs, pulling the trunk.

Must be her dad, Penny thought as she turned toward the room mother's apartment Mrs. Gibson had pointed out to her that morning. When she knocked, Mrs. Gibson opened the door.

"Hi, Penny, did your roommate get in? How's it going?"

Penny burst into tears and Mrs. Gibson drew her into her room and listened to Penny's tale of the repulsive roommate.

"She's just awful! She doesn't want a roommate, she doesn't like the room, she doesn't like the dresser liners, and she doesn't like me!"

Mrs. Gibson felt sick for this young girl whose heart was so open to others. How anyone could reject Penny was unbelievable.

"I'm so sorry. I wish I could do something to get you a different roommate. I'll talk to the dean but don't count on it."

Mrs. Gibson handed Penny a tissue and Penny wiped her tears while the dorm mother engaged her in conversation about her upcoming classes and plans for running for the student council. Finally calm, Penny thanked Mrs. Gibson for listening and spent the rest of the afternoon visiting her friends and meeting other new students.

Many of the girls had changed their appearance over the summer with new hairstyles and makeup. Some came with tales of summer boyfriends. Several had thrilling vacation stories. Penny eagerly listened to everything and lived vicariously through each experience.

Going back to her room, Penny entered to find Courtney alone amidst a half dozen boxes and suitcases. A vanity table had been added to the room's furnishings. Determined to be nice no matter how she was treated, Penny took a deep breath and initiated a conversation.

"Your mother and father are gone?"

"Mother and father? You mean, Jack? He's the limo driver. Dad has to be in Washington this week. He's a United States Senator. Yea, Mom is gone. You've heard of hit and run? This was dump and run. She dumped me here and hit the road."

Penny heard bitterness in Courtney's voice and saw scorn on her face. Penny suddenly felt sorry for her. Even when her parents left her with her aunt and uncle to chase the carnival circuit, Penny never felted dumped anywhere.

"I'm sorry you feel dumped here. You didn't want to come to

Charlotte Hills?"

"No. I wanted to go to school in Switzerland but Daddy said the daughter of a United States Senator had to go to an American prep school. And since he is the senator from *the great state of North Carolina,* it has to be here."

Courtney's sarcastic emphasis about North Carolina made Penny smile. This roommate certainly changed moods quickly.

"I'm sure Switzerland would have been great, but Charlotte Hills is a wonderful school. The teachers are great. Most of the girls who graduate get into the best colleges. I think you'll like it if you give it a chance. We can be friends if you give me a chance."

Penny held her breath and waited for another sarcastic remark, but, instead, Courtney switched moods again and turned on the charm.

"How sweet you are. Maybe you can help me put my clothes away." Courtney schmoozed. "I tried not to pack too many clothes but I just couldn't decide what to bring. I know there are uniforms for class but I'll be out of them and into my real clothes as often as possible."

Penny was relieved that Courtney was actually talking to her. Maybe they could get along after all.

"I'll be glad to help. If you need more dresser drawers or closet space, I have some. I only need space for my uniforms, church dresses, and a few skirts and blouses. You can have the rest."

"Church dresses? Do we have to go to church here?"

"No. But there is a school bus that takes the girls who want to go to a local church on Sundays. I hope maybe you'll come with me one Sunday. I think you would like it."

"Don't count on it. The limo will be coming to take me home every weekend. Anyway, maybe you've not heard - God is dead."

Courtney's pronouncement, stated emphatically like it had been Cronkite's lead story on the CBS Evening News, startled Penny.

"That's not funny, Courtney."

"I didn't mean it to be funny. The notion that God is alive and cares about anything is passé. Trust me, Penny. You've been locked up in this school for a long time. Out in the real world, we know

15

God is dead - if he was ever alive at all."

Anger began to swell in Penny. The hope of a roommate who would be compatible spiritually was blown out of the water. Not only was Courtney not a Christian, she was an atheist!

Penny turned away from Courtney, gazed upward and silently mouthed, *"Help me."* Calmness entered her spirit as she turned and looked at Courtney. This girl was so in need of God's love. Penny suddenly realized why she was Courtney's roommate and remembered Mrs. Gibson's advice from early that morning. Penny was going to live her faith in front of Courtney. Her roommate would see God alive and well and working miracles all around her.

Penny smiled at Courtney.

"It's almost supper time. Show me what you want me to do to help. Then I'll take you down to the dining room and introduce you to everybody. I know you will love it here."

In twenty minutes, everything was put away, and the two girls went downstairs to spend their last evening before the 1964-65 school term began.

3

> Better is a little with the fear of the LORD,
> than great treasure with trouble.
> Proverbs 15:16

Charlotte Hills Academy was established as a liberal arts preparatory school for young ladies from white, wealthy, east coast families. Perched in rolling hills twenty miles west of Charlotte, North Carolina, the school opened in 1872 with twenty-seven resident girls in the secondary program and forty girls in the primary day school through 8th grade. The original building had three stories; administration on the first floor, classrooms on the second, and dormitory rooms on the third. Through the years, two dormitory buildings, a classroom and library building and a gymnasium/auditorium were constructed in a quadrangle near the original building that now held administrative operations. In 1964 the residents numbered two hundred twenty three with sixty-five other girls commuting as day students from the immediate area. Charlotte Hills Academy remained segregated and white only.

The first day of school was Wednesday after Labor Day. The girls scurried through the day and got their first taste of new schedules, classes, courses, and teachers. As Mrs. Gibson predicted, Penny had most of her classes with Courtney. Both girls were academically talented but there the comparison ended. Courtney, loath to open her books, made superior grades regardless. Penny also made excellent grades but spent hours in her textbooks every evening and worked diligently on homework.

Courtney exhibited her best behavior in class. Her parents had promised a vacation in Rio de Janeiro for Christmas if she could get through a semester without trouble. It was just the incentive for a girl who was very sensual in her appetites. Her appearance belied her almost sixteen years. Incensed about school rules regarding clothing, hair, and makeup, Courtney walked a wobbly line between compliance and rebellion. The promise to Penny to wear the uniforms only as absolutely necessary was not an empty one. Her clothes worn in the dorm were extremely flashy as was her hair and makeup. Courtney tried to get Penny to let her make up her face but Penny just laughed her off. She tried not to express condemnation nor approval of Courtney. Penny's life was a simple one. Other than her uncle, the priorities of her life were her relationship with God and education. She saw no need of extravagance even when offered to her.

Mrs. Gibson checked on Penny every day. Sometimes it was in the dining room or in the hall between classes. On the first Friday afternoon of the term, she stopped by Penny's dorm room to say hello. Courtney, preparing to go home for the weekend, was suspicious the dorm mother's frequent visits were an attempt to catch Courtney out of compliance with school rules.

"Where does she get off walking in on us so much?" Courtney complained to Penny when the dorm mother left the room after a short visit.

"Who? Mrs. Gibson? She doesn't just walk in. She always knocks and I invite her in. She has been wonderful to me—like a real mother. She is also a good friend. Don't you like her?"

"No, I don't. She must not have a lot going on in her life for her to have a bunch of teenage girls for friends. And she lives here, doesn't she? Why is she not living with her husband?"

Penny bit her lip while deciding how to respond.

"Courtney, Mrs. Gibson is a wonderful woman. She has a degree in social work and owned a successful business before she came to Charlotte Hills after her husband died. She is real quality."

Courtney, surprised at the ardent defense her roommate gave the dorm mother, was delighted to get some background on the woman who she considered a threat. She decided to back away from her criticism of her roommate's mentor.

"Really? Maybe I've misjudged her. I know she's all you've got."

"O.K. But she's not all I've got. I have my uncle. He's my legal guardian. You haven't met him yet. He works for the school. We have Sunday dinners together after church. I'd love for you to meet him."

"Your uncle? Wow. No wonder Mrs. Gibson pays you so much attention. If my guardian was an administrator for the school, she would want to be my best friend, too."

"Oh, he's not an administrator. He is one of the janitors."

Courtney's jaw dropped and she started howling.

"A janitor! Your guardian is the school janitor! No wonder you're called Penny—you're not worth much!"

Penny, stunned at the sudden verbal attack, caught her breath. What was wrong with this girl? In a sudden surge of courage, Penny got up from her desk and stepped right up into a startled Courtney's face. Her eyes were focused and her words calm and deliberate.

"Courtney, despite our differences I have accepted you and tried to be your friend. You may think you have everything and I have nothing but I have people in my life who love me unconditionally. I also have the very alive and real Lord in my life and with Him, I have more than you could ever imagine. I feel very sorry for you."

That said, Penny turned and walked out the door, leaving a stunned Courtney wondering how sweet little Penny had mustered up the nerve to stand up to her. She was going to have to reevaluate the strategies she was using to put her roommate in her pocket.

4

> "A man's pride shall bring him low:
> but honor shall uphold the humble in spirit."
> Proverbs 29:23

Penny didn't return to her dorm room that night, instead going to Rebecca Gibson, the woman Penny turned to at the first sign of trouble or concern, much as she supposed most of the girls at Charlotte Hills did with their own mothers.

Penny told the dorm mother what happened and, despite the fact that Courtney would be gone for the weekend, asked permission to go to her uncle's apartment for the night. The dorm mother escorted her to the administration building basement and, with Penny safely in her uncle's sitting room, she and Baron Sanford spoke in hushed tones in the stairwell.

"Rebecca, how could you let this happen? That Courtney is vicious. I don't want to be an embarrassment to Penny. She deserves so much more! I want to give her so much more!"

Rebecca put her hand on Baron's shoulder. They had become good friends through the years and a tenderness was growing between the two that gave Rebecca pause to imagine herself in a romantic relationship for the first time in over ten years.

"Penny is a strong girl and knows she is loved. It doesn't matter to her if you are the school janitor or a Rockefeller. You are an honorable man, Baron Sanford! God will bless you for that. You give her everything she needs. Most important, you are grounding her in faith that will sustain her all her life. Material riches come and go but her faith, Baron, her faith will last for eternity."

Baron looked into the face of the only woman beside his Helen he ever had feelings for. He reached up and took her hand from his shoulder, grasping it with gentleness.

"You're right, Rebecca. I shouldn't blame you. I have to encourage her to think spiritually right now. But she just turned sixteen. How much can I hope she can deal with?"

"I think she showed tonight that she can deal with a lot! She stood up and rebuked that girl and had the courage to walk out on her. I'm proud of her."

Baron nodded and hand in hand walked Rebecca up the stairs to the basement entrance of the administration building. Stepping onto the sidewalk, the two paused comfortably holding hands and continued their conversation.

"Thank you, Rebecca, for taking care of Penny. I don't know what I would do if you weren't here to watch out for her."

Rebecca's hand felt warm in Baron's. She gazed into his face, unaware that a limo was slowly driving toward the campus gates with a girl in the rear, searching the scene eagerly to see who Mrs. Gibson was having a cozy moment with.

"Interesting….I must do some snooping when I get back," she mused.

After saying their goodnights, Baron watched Rebecca cross the campus to Bryant Hall. Seeing her enter the building, he returned to his little suite of rooms to find Penny asleep on the couch. Baron pulled a blanket off his bed and covered his niece, watching her sweet face and remembering when she first came into his life.

#####

Baron and Helen Sanford were childless. While he poured his disappointment out of a beer bottle every night, Helen turned to the Lord and trusted Him to give her a child according to His will. One day her brother came to their door.

"Helen, Sylvia and I have been offered a job managing a new carnival. We will be traveling most of the year and since Penny is ready to start school, we wondered if you and Baron would take her in."

Helen had been excited about Penny living with them but Baron resented the intrusion into their lives.

"Helen, she's not ours. We can barely support ourselves on this land."

"But Baron, you know how sweet she is. Tom and Sylvia need our help. He's promised to give us twenty dollars a month. That would help, won't it?"

Looking back, Baron felt shame that he agreed to take Penny because of the money. As the weeks went by, the joy Penny brought to their home changed him. Baron stopped drinking and

21

put his energies into his small farm. It was starting to make a profit and the family was happy. Then came the spring of '56 and the storm that would bring life and death changes to the community.

Once the debris was cleared, some families decided to rebuild. But Baron had lost too much. Not only was Helen gone and her entire family, but his parents had also been killed. Finding a buyer for his now empty land, Baron purchased a '55 Ford coupe and he and Penny moved to Charlotte.

John Lawson, manager of the Piggy Wiggly, was a Christian man. When Baron walked into his office looking for a job, he listened to his story with compassion and made a job for him. He and his wife also helped him find a small apartment near an elementary school for Penny. Over the next few months, he watched Baron prove to be an honest, dependable, and hard worker, willing to do anything asked of him. When he read in the paper that Charlotte Hills Academy was opening an additional dormitory and expanding its staff, he used his connection as one of the school's vendors and called the headmaster, telling him about Baron Sanford. They agreed to meet with him and, with great hope, John called Baron into his office and sent him to Charlotte Hills with a glowing letter of recommendation.

Baron could not believe his fortune. The compensation offered him for the janitor position included a small basement apartment and meals for himself and Penny, classes for Penny, and a small salary. Moving to Charlotte Hills, they began their new life.

Shortly after their arrival, Rebecca Gibson came to Baron and asked his permission for Penny to ride the bus with other girls to the local Baptist church.

"Mr. Sanford, I'd like to take Penny to church with me. Would that be all right with you?"

"I guess. If she wants to."

"How about you? Would you like to come along?"

"Oh, no. Church stuff has never been for me. You can take Penny but I'd like her back in time to have lunch with me."

Rebecca agreed but, ironically a few weeks later, the school assigned Baron the responsibility to drive the bus. He and Penny sat together each Sunday, Penny relishing the music and messages and Baron coming under conviction more and more each week. On the first Sunday in November, both he and Penny made professions of faith and were baptized. Now their new life included the Lord! Shortly after, Baron and Penny made a holiday trip to the cemetery and put flowers on the family graves. With tears streaming down his face, Baron stood at Helen's gravestone and told her that he would see her again.

Baron's life was rich. He thanked the Lord daily for work he loved, his home, and Penny. She was his joy. He would do anything for this child! Now, watching her sleep on his couch, he remembered he was not the only one who cared about Penny. Baron went to his knees, laid his hands on Penny's shoulder as she slept and prayed for God to protect and help the child they both loved and particularly deliver her from every storm of life, including the storm of Courtney.

5

Penny stayed with her uncle that weekend and after Baron had driven the bus back to the school on Sunday, he put Penny in their old '55 Ford to go to town for dinner. Eating together was a treat they looked forward to each Sunday. Many of the girls went home for the weekend and the few that didn't were served soup and sandwiches by a skeleton kitchen staff. Sometimes Penny and Uncle Baron ate in the dining hall with the girls but often they went to town to look for little diners where they enjoyed choosing from a menu.

Baron started the car and turned on the heater to dispel the chill of the early fall day. As the engine idled, he asked Penny to scoot to the center of the seat, got out and went around to the passenger door and opened it. Suddenly, Mrs. Gibson appeared and slid in beside her.

"I hope you don't mind if I join you and your uncle for lunch," the dorm mother said with a grin.

"Oh, no, I don't mind at all! I'm happy to see you, Mrs. Gibson. I enjoyed your solo this morning at church. I was going to tell you when I got back to the dorm this evening."

"Thank you, Penny."

Baron got back into the car and offered an explanation to his niece.

"Penny, Mrs. Gibson has been such a good friend to both of us and I thought it would be nice if I took you two ladies to lunch today. Is that all right with you?"

Penny grinned and put her left arm through the crook in her uncle's arm and grabbed Mrs. Gibson's hand with her right hand.

"Why, Uncle Bear! I can't think of any place I'd rather be than between the two of you!"

"All right then. How about that little Italian restaurant on the highway. Is that all right with you, Rebecca?"

24

"Sounds wonderful, Baron."

Penny sat back and closed her eyes. *They were calling each other by their first names! They sounded so familiar with one another! How long had this been going on?* Penny began writing in her naïve mind a fairy tale romance between the two that sat beside her that ended with the three of them living happily ever after.

The afternoon was all Penny hoped it would be. For the first time, Penny had no pang of longing at seeing children with two parents. Uncle Bear and Mrs. Gibson weren't her mother and father but she knew they loved her. The chatter and laughter they enjoyed was no different than the other families sitting around them.

"You girls order what you want. The main dishes come with salad and breadsticks. One of the men I work with said the lasagna is wonderful."

Each entrée on the menu was contemplated. Rebecca explained the term "Florentine" causing Baron to panic that he had almost ordered a dish with spinach. They laughed it off and Penny decided that she would order it and convince her uncle to try one bite. That didn't work but the three enjoyed the attempt.

"What are you going to have, Mrs. Gibson?"

"I think I'll have the Chicken Gnocchi Veronica. It is a chicken and vegetable dish with gnocchi and cheese sauce."

"What's gnocchi, Uncle Bear?"

Baron shrugged and rolled his eyes playfully.

Mrs. Gibson laughed. "Gnocchi is the Italian word for dumplings."

"Oh. I like dumplings. Remember, Uncle Bear, the chicken and dumplings Aunt Helen made?"

Penny and her uncle shared a smile as they both thought back to the life they shared so long ago.

Baron decided on the recommended lasagna. A moment after the order was made, a large bowl of salad and chilled plates were placed on the table as well as a basket of hot breadsticks.

"Rebecca, would you please serve the salad plates after I give thanks?"

She nodded and the three circled the table with their hands

while Baron prayed.

"Heavenly Father, We love you and thank you for your presence and guidance in our lives. We are blessed to be in your love and care and ask you to show us your will, individually and jointly, for our lives. Thank you for this food. We ask you to bless it to our bodies as we present our bodies to you in your service. In Jesus name, Amen."

Dropping hands, Rebecca busily served the salad. Penny watched their interaction as they gleefully bantered about the hot peppers she tried to put on his plate. Uncle Bear had prayed for God's will individually and jointly. Something was definitely going on between these two. Penny choked back a giggle and grabbed a breadstick to keep from erupting with joy.

After a drive in the country and a stop at an ice cream parlor for dessert, the three returned to Charlotte Hills late in the afternoon. Rebecca and Penny said goodbye to Baron and walked the short distance from the parking lot to Bryant Hall. Rebecca reverted to her dorm mother role and prepared Penny for resuming her roommate status with Courtney.

"Penny, you remember who and what you are. You are Penny Wilburn, a Charlotte Hills student with all the rights and privileges as anyone else, including Courtney Guilford. You have always treated her with respect and I know will continue to do so. Expect her to treat you with respect. If she doesn't, tell me but don't confront her. I will deal with her for the school and we will both pray she will see the need of the Lord in her life."

As the two entered the front door, Courtney jumped up from one of the lobby chairs and rushed to Penny.

"Oh, I'm so glad to see you, Penny. I was worried about you! Where did you find her, Mrs. Gibson?"

"Find her? She wasn't lost, Courtney. We just spent a lovely afternoon together. Now you girls go on to your room. I hear you both have a history paper that you have to turn in an outline for tomorrow."

"Yes, ma'am. I did mine before the limo picked me up. Mom and I flew to New York and did some shopping. Can't wait to show you my new clothes, Penny," Courtney responded, linking her arm with Penny's and moving toward the stairs.

Penny looked back at Mrs. Gibson as she was led away. Mrs. Gibson winked at her. Watching the two of them disappear at the top of the stairs, she turned to go to her own room. Courtney was too friendly and attentive to Penny. She was up to something!

In their room, Penny changed her clothes into a simple skirt and sweater then went to her desk. Although she always left it tidy, it seemed a big disheveled. Penny turned to Courtney.

"Courtney, did you use my desk?"

"Oh, yea. Mine was a mess and I sat there to write my outline."

"Courtney, I've offered you my dresser drawers and my closet. But my desk is off limits. I hope you remember that in the future!"

"Gees, Penny. Stop the world and I'll get off!"

Penny turned back to her desk, put it in order and began reviewing the index cards that held her research notes. Courtney, in a gray poodle skirt and tight hot pink sweater, sat in the middle of her bed and browsed through movie star magazines. She suddenly started squealing and jumped up, shoving the magazine in Penny's face.

"Look, Penny, Annette Funicello has on the same outfit I do! Can you believe that? I'm going to go show the other girls the magazine picture. Don't work too hard."

Courtney left the room and Penny turned back to her work. She spent the next hour carefully writing the outline with her ink pen. Her subject was Helen Keller. Penny had read two biographies, a Life magazine feature, and two different encyclopedia articles on the blind woman. Her index cards were printed clearly and well organized, making the outline easy to put together. She had worked hard on this paper. It was the first one of her junior year and she wanted to do well. She knew she was at Charlotte Hills because of her uncle's job and she was grateful for the opportunity but she would need straight As to have hopes of a college scholarship.

The outline done, Penny left the paper on her desk to dry completely and went to the bathroom to wash up for supper. Walking in the door, she immediately noticed a strong cigarette smell. Under one of the stalls, Penny detected the bottom edge of a grey skirt.

"Courtney, is that you?"

The sound of the toilet flushing preceded the opening of the door and emergence of Courtney in a fog of smoke.

"Courtney! You can't smoke in here! You shouldn't be smoking at all!"

"Oh, don't be a baby. I've been smoking for over a year." Courtney pulled a cologne bottle out of her purse and pumped a mist around herself and the air in the bathroom. The combination of smoke and cologne sent Penny into a coughing spell.

Finally catching her breath, Penny glared at Courtney and went into a stall at the far end of the room. *She calls me a baby? She's the one sucking on a cigarette like a pacifier!* Exiting the toilet stall, Penny realized Courtney had left the restroom. Never mind the name calling and disrespect. Penny had a duty to the school to report the smoking. She was very well aware of the student code of ethics that applied. She had to turn her roommate in. If the last week had been difficult, the next week would be impossible.

#####

Penny wanted people to like her and most did. When she was little, she was teased by other children because her family was poor. When the carnival was in town, her parents worked it. One day, her mother gave her some tickets to give to a few of the children but her father got mad when he found out and made Penny get the tickets back. Young Penny was humiliated and avoided her playmates after that, withdrawing into herself and the small world she made in her home.

But home was not easy either. Her mother and father lived a rough life with frequent parties with something she heard Uncle Bear call "reefer." At first, she was sent to her grandparents who lived down the road to spend the night while her parents entertained. One night, she saw Grandpa grab Grandma by her hair and throw her against the wall.

"Grandpa, stop!" Five-year-old Penny ran to help her grandmother.

"She can take it, little girl, she's taken lots worst and deserved every beaten'! Get away from her if you don't want to get hurt!"

Penny didn't get hurt but her grandmother went to the hospital with broken ribs and a concussion. Grandpa spent a few days in jail. From then on, Penny's mother sent her to Aunt Helen's during their parties. Uncle Bear drank but was a quiet and sad drunk who fell asleep on the couch every night surrounded by beer bottles. Aunt Helen entertained Penny by baking cookies and reading to her.

Then came the day Penny's dad asked his sister and Baron to take Penny full time while they joined the carnival year round. Penny started first grade and before long was reading stories to Aunt Helen. She and Aunt Helen went to church and Penny got her first Bible. Penny asked a lot of questions about God and Helen answered her as simply as she could, telling her young niece God loved her and would always take care of her. Penny wanted to believe in God. She started to say prayers at the dinner table with Aunt Helen and pray at night when she went to bed. But then the tornado came. How could God love and care about her when He let a tornado take so much away from her?

Going back to church after moving to Charlotte Hills rekindled the spiritual seeds planted in Penny by her Aunt Helen. Her sweet and quiet personality provided rich soil for her belief to grow and, supported by Uncle Bear who also had come to believe in Jesus, Penny made her profession of faith.

As she matured through her years at Charlotte Hills Academy, Penny's personality became more confident but she never lost her sweetness. Believing it always more beneficial to be nice, she helped the other girls work through conflicts and had become a leader in student life. Each year she had served as a representative on the student council and now that she was a junior, she was eligible to serve as an officer. She had already written the essay she needed for her candidacy for student council recording secretary and planned on turning in her application on Monday. Serving would be a good learning experience for her and help her enhance her transcript for college applications. It was also something she believed the Lord wanted her to do. More than anything, Penny wanted to please the Lord but it wasn't always easy pleasing the Lord and people, too. Turning Courtney in for smoking certainly would not please her roommate or Courtney's circle of friends. And how would that effect the election?

Penny looked in the mirror and prayed the person looking back at her would have the courage to do the right thing.

6

> "No weapon that is formed against thee shall prosper; and every
> tongue that shall rise against thee in judgment thou salt condemn.
> This is the heritage of the servants of the LORD,
> and their righteousness is of me, saith the LORD."
> Isaiah 54:17

Penny went to the dining hall crowded with girls returned from their weekend visits home. Sunday evening was spaghetti night at Charlotte Hills and the girls enjoyed the atmosphere of reunion and hearing about everyone's weekend adventures.

Penny noticed the giggling crowd around Courtney. Penny shook off the feeling they were talking about her and went through the serving line by herself and sat down to eat. Bowing her head, Penny gave thanks for her food and raised her head to see her friend, Julia, sitting across from her.

"Hi, Julia. Did you have a nice weekend?"

"Yea, I did. Hear you were gone, too."

"I spent the weekend with my uncle. We had a nice visit. Went on a drive to see the fall leaves."

"That's nice. Um, I heard you had a big fight with Courtney and that's why you left the dorm."

"A fight? No. Is that what Courtney is saying?"

"Yea. She said you yelled at her and called her a bad name."

"What? Do you believe her? Do you believe I did that?"

"Penny, I've never heard you raise your voice to anyone. And I don't think you even know any bad names!"

Penny smiled. Julia was a good friend. She had a lot of good friends at school. But Courtney was flashy and exciting, giving the boarding school girls vicarious experiences they would normally never have. It was obvious Courtney was trying to influence these girls. Penny didn't want her friends to have to choose between her and Courtney but if that's what Courtney was setting up, Penny could only be herself and trust that her true friends would recognize the lies Courtney told.

"Thanks, Julia. I'm trying hard to be a friend to Courtney.

How you doing with your roommate?"

"Oh, great! Karen and I have so much in common. She's a Christian and likes to read Grace Livingston Hill like I do!"

"Aren't they great? Have you read *Mary Arden,* her last book? It was so good! Did you know Mrs. Gibson has a big collection of Grace Livingston Hill books?"

"She does? Hey, wouldn't it be great to have a Grace Livingston Hill Book Club? I bet lots of girls would enjoy reading them. Maybe even Courtney would get her head out of her movie magazines and read one."

Penny smiled but didn't say anything. She was tempted to be critical of Courtney but bit her lip. Uncle Bear had reminded her just that weekend, "Let her do all the ugly."

"I like the idea of a book club. I'll ask Mrs. Gibson if she will let us use her books."

Penny and Julia drifted into meaningless chatter about the spaghetti sauce, the weather, and the new P.E. uniforms. They put up their trays and separated, Julia going up the stairs to the dorm rooms and Penny heading toward Mrs. Gibson's room. She had to talk to her about Courtney's smoking.

Rebecca Gibson answered the knock on her door.

"Hello, Penny. Come in."

"Mrs. Gibson, I need to tell you something about Courtney. I don't want to tattle but she has broken a pretty big rule. She was smoking in the bathroom upstairs."

Mrs. Gibson shook her head.

"Oh, my. That is big. Was anybody else there?"

"No, just me. It was right before supper."

"Umm. I wish someone else had seen it. Courtney could say you are lying to get her in trouble."

"I don't lie, Mrs. Gibson."

"I know that, Penny. Everybody knows that. But Courtney's family doesn't know you and they are likely to fight against any charges brought against Courtney. They will ask for proof and we don't have any."

"Maybe Courtney will admit it."

"Maybe. But if she lies, I'm afraid her parents will believe her."

"So, what do I do?"

"You go to Dean Merrick tomorrow morning and tell him what happened, when it happened, and where it happened. Let him know that you are reporting it because of the student code of ethics. Don't talk about any of the other problems you are having with her. Just give him the facts without any judgments."

"Yes, ma'am."

"And Penny, you be careful. Courtney has an agenda. I'm not sure what it is but I'm afraid you are in her way. Would you like me to pray with you about this?"

"Oh, yes!"

The two knelt down next to the small sofa. Penny prayed and asked God to help her be strong against the temptation to be angry with Courtney. Rebecca asked God to guide Penny and help her trust Him to work everything out for her good. She also prayed for Courtney.

"Lord, Courtney needs to believe in you. Please open her eyes to see you clearly and know how much you love her."

The two said goodnight and Penny left. The dorm mother went to her desk and recorded notes about the visit from Penny. Having been a keeper of journals since her teenage years, she knew the importance of writing things down as soon as possible after their occurrence. Since she had been at Charlotte Hills in the role of dorm mother, it had helped on more than one occasion to have notes about conversations and confrontations with students, staff, and parents. She already had several anecdotal notes about Courtney. She prayed she would not have to use them to protect Penny.

Penny went to her room and opened the door. Courtney was sprawled on the floor making posters.

"There you are. You certainly disappear a lot!"

Courtney stood up and held up one of the posters.

"I'm running for student council recording secretary! How do you like my posters?"

Penny's jaw dropped.

"When did you decide to do that?"

"At supper. We were talking about the student council election and one of the girls suggested I run. Since I'm just a junior, I can only run for recording secretary. I thought I'd get started on my campaign. Do you know who else is running?"

Penny bit her lip. "Not really. You have to turn in your application by Tuesday morning. The faculty will select two girls for each office. The ballot will be posted on Wednesday. I guess we'll find out then."

"You're tight with Mrs. Gibson. Do you think you can find out before Wednesday?"

"No," Penny stated emphatically. Suddenly, she wanted to crawl under her quilt and hide.

"I'm going to bed. Are you going to need the overhead light much longer?"

"No. You can turn it off. I'll just use my bed lamp while I brainstorm some speech ideas."

"Thanks. Goodnight, Courtney."

"Nite, roomy," Courtney replied, her eyes twinkling with amusement that she had pulled one over on priggish Penny.

7

Charlotte Hills dormitories had bells that rang at 6 o'clock each
morning. Penny was so accustomed to the schedule she would
naturally wake before the bell. She was the first in the shower and
back in her room getting dressed before most of the girls crawled
out of their beds. Once in her uniform, Penny would get her Bible
and read. The first morning after Courtney arrived, Penny was
taunted so much about reading a Bible that she now went
downstairs to the lobby where she had her Bible reading and
prayer time in peaceful solitude.

After her quiet time, Penny went to the dining room for
breakfast. Julia was there as well as Mary Ann, Linda, and Janice,
the girls Penny had roomed with at Mason Hall. The girls happily
chatted about their weekend.

Mary Ann asked, "Have you heard Courtney is going to run
for recording secretary?"

Julia gasped and looked at Penny.

"I thought you were going to apply for that job, Penny?"

"I am," Penny replied.

"Does Courtney know that?"

"I never told her but she may have seen my application in my
desk drawer."

"That's evil! I bet she's only running because you are! You've
been preparing for that job for six years. She's only been here one
week and she wants to take the job away from you!"

"Hey, calm down. If she wants to run, that's fine. I'm up for a
good contest."

"You are too nice, Penny Wilburn! Well, you have my vote."

"Mine, too." Mary Ann added. She turned to the other girls.
"Tell her, Janice."

"Got to go," said Janice.

"Me, too," Linda uttered under her breath. Both girls stepped

35

away quickly. Julia and Mary Ann looked at each other.

"Huh! You won't need them. Penny, you turn that application in and we'll be your campaign managers. I've got poster board and paint. We'll get started today. Right, Mary Ann?"

Mary Ann nodded.

Penny's mind reviewed the time line of the last twenty-four hours. She returned from her weekend and found her desk disturbed. Before supper, she discovered Courtney smoking in the bathroom. After supper, Courtney told Penny she was going to run for recording secretary. By breakfast, other girls in the dorm knew she was running. The battle lines were being drawn.

Penny thought about the prayer she had prayed the night before in Mrs. Gibson's room. She had asked God to keep her from being angry with Courtney. Seemed like she was getting more and more reason to be angry. Was God hearing her?

"We'll talk about it later. Time to go to class," Penny answered. The girls headed upstairs to get their books and begin their school day.

By the first Monday of the school term, classes were in full swing. History was Penny's first period class and the outline for the first term paper was due today. Penny had worked hard on her Helen Keller paper and she was pleased with it. She was good at writing, very analytical in the way she put papers together. Getting an A on this paper would be an excellent way to commence her junior year grade point average.

Once the papers were turned in, Mrs. Grayson began lecturing on 20th century history. Penny took laborious notes, focusing all her attention on the teacher. Sitting on the other side of the room, Courtney jotted down ideas for her student council campaign speech. She knew Penny also wanted the job having found her application essay in the top drawer of Penny's desk. Snooping had always served Courtney well. Her own mother only had control over what her daughter permitted since Courtney had discovered letters from the husband of her mother's best friend, letters that showed the husband was on a much more intimate standing than he should have been. Mrs. Guilford loved being a senator's wife and negotiated with Courtney to keep her dalliance private. Courtney got a Bahamas trip out of that snoop.

At the end of the first period, Penny went to Dean Derrick's office and turned in her application for student council. She also requested an appointment with the dean for her typing class period right after lunch. She went on to her second period class with trepidation, knowing that there was no turning back. She was going to report Courtney's smoking.

At lunch, Courtney ate with her entourage, engaging everyone with stories about her frequent visits to the capital and the White House, including the time she met the First Lady Jacqueline Kennedy and played with Caroline. Courtney claimed her mother was a friend and confident of Mrs. Kennedy and Courtney said she knew things about the case only the most important people in the country knew. Of course, she was not at liberty to say what those things were but claimed the experience made her more than qualified to be an officer on the student council.

On the other side of the cafeteria, Penny and Julia ate together and talked about the election as well.

"I don't even know if I'm going to be accepted as a candidate. Courtney is the daughter of a U.S. Senator! She's certainly going to be competition. Do you know who else is applying?" Penny asked.

The two girls talked about those in the student body who might be running for the various offices. Finishing their lunch, they took their trays back to the kitchen. Penny looked back at Courtney as she headed toward the exit and her meeting with the dean. This was it. God knew her motives were right. But there still might be serious consequences to pay.

8

Penny sat in the outer office of the Dean and took deep breaths to calm herself. She had never had to tattle on somebody before and the idea was quite distasteful to her. But it was her duty and obligation to report wrongdoing. Mrs. Gibson understood and Dean Warrick would understand too.

Dean Warrick came to his door and called Penny's name.

"Hello, Miss Wilburn. It's good to see you. How is your uncle?"

"He's well, Sir. We spent the weekend together and went for a drive in the country. The leaves are turning early this year."

The dean sat on the edge of his desk in front of Penny. "Yes, they are. Well, Penny, tell me what brought you to see me."

Penny took a final deep breath.

"Well, Sir. I have been on the student council as a representative for several years. I know the importance of the code of honor and have never had an occasion to bring any report of student wrongdoing to you. Until today."

The dean stood up and went around his desk and sat down. He pulled out a piece of paper and scribbled something at the top.

"Please continue," Dean Warrick answered.

"Last evening, just before supper, I finished some homework and went to the bathroom on the second floor of Bryant Hall where I live. When I walked into the bathroom, I smelled cigarettes and a fog of smoke filled the air. A girl was inside a stall. The toilet flushed and she came out. I told her she shouldn't be smoking and she said she had been smoking for more than a year. Then she sprayed cologne on her clothes and left the bathroom."

Dean Merrick wrote quickly as Penny narrated the event. Looking up finally, he asked the necessary question.

"What was her name?"

With sudden tears in her eyes, Penny blurted out, "Courtney

Guilford, my roommate."

Dean Merrick scribbled something, dropped his pen, and leaned back in his chair.

"Courtney Guilford. Well, Penny, thank you for bringing this to my attention. Who else knows about it?"

"Just Mrs. Gibson. She told me to come to you."

"Does Courtney know about this meeting?"

"No, Sir. I don't think so."

"All right. Let's keep all this to ourselves. I'll take care of everything. Ask Mrs. Tucker for a pass back to class."

Penny left the dean's office relieved. She picked up her pass and scurried into what was left of her typing class.

Dean Merrick stared at the name on the paper in front of him. The ramifications of bringing a charge against the daughter of Senator Martin Guilford were huge. Despite a history of suspensions and expulsions, Courtney Guilford was accepted at Charlotte Hills Academy when a $40,000 donation was offered to the Charlotte Hills Foundation. The Guilford's stipulated the money not be publicized, fearing the knowledge of the donation would give the perception they were buying admission which in effect they were.

The dean pressed his intercom. "Sybil, please connect me to President Garvin then find Rebecca Gibson and ask her to come to my office."

A moment later, the secretary buzzed back that President Garvin was on the phone.

"Phil, we have a situation. It's about the Guilford girl…."

#####

Penny finished her last class of the day and went to the library to select a book to do a book report on. As she scanned the titles looking for something of interest, she heard low voices on the other side of the stack.

"Here's your 25, Kerry. The outline looked great. I need the first draft by next Monday. It needs to be typed, double spaced, and 750 words. Can you handle that?"

"If you can handle another 25, I can. Then, remember I get 50 for the final draft. 100 dollars for a history paper is a good deal."

"I remember. You remember that this is just between you and

39

me. You don't want to double cross me."

"Nor you, me. I'll have the paper at supper next Sunday. Meet me here same time next Monday to pay me."

Penny heard the shuffling of steps on the terrazzo floor. She held her breath and tiptoed away from the area. Courtney was buying her history report! Penny knew Kerry Andrews. She and Penny had been in English together the last two years. Kerry was an excellent writer and very prolific writing research papers. She had never been friendly to Penny, treating her as a competitor in the classroom. But Penny had never imagined Kerry as someone who would be involved in cheating. Courtney was another matter. She didn't put any indiscretion past her roommate and was not surprised that the paper Courtney had said she did before she left for the weekend was actually being done by someone else for money. Now Penny wondered what Courtney was doing at her desk if she wasn't writing her paper.

Penny slipped further into the stacks. She saw Courtney saunter through the library and finally leave. After Courtney left, Penny checked her book out and went to her room. Courtney was there, putting nail polish on her toenails.

"Hi, roomy!" Courtney greeted cheerfully.

"Hi, Courtney. I'm going to start working on my rough draft tonight, how about you?"

"Oh, yea. It's the next thing on my schedule after I get my toes done."

"I'm writing about Helen Keller. I never asked you what your topic was."

"Eleanor Roosevelt. Did you know she was a cousin of my grandmother?"

"Really? Your mother or father's side?"

"Mother's."

"Were you able to add any personal material to your paper?"

"No. I just used the normal sources."

"I'm sure Mrs. Belford would allow it."

"We'll, um, it's too late now. The outline's been turned in."

Courtney finished putting polish on her toes, grabbed a notebook and began writing, her feet hanging off the bed with tissues stuffed between her toes. Penny went to her desk and began working on a draft of her own paper, carefully following her outline. She glanced over at Courtney several times and wondered what she was doing while pretending to work on a paper she was paying Kerry one hundred dollars to write!

Penny had known of several students cheating through the years. She remembered Jane Kenner with spelling words stuffed up her sweater sleeve. The teacher caught her during a test and gave her a zero for the test and a week's detention. There was also Sue Tyler who copied Eve Cooper's geography homework. Both girls got additional work and a week's detention. Detention was no picnic at Charlotte Hills. It was held in the dean's outer office with Mrs. Tucker who ran detention with strict no-nonsense rules against talking, sleeping, reading, or working on anything except the essay she gave you to keep you writing the entire ninety minute detention period. It had to be finished by the end of the period or you stayed until it was. Then when you went back to your room, you still had your homework to do. No, detention usually was a real deterrent to breaking the rules at Charlotte Hills. But, Penny supposed, not to Courtney.

The Charlotte Hills Student Code of Ethics loomed like a thick cloud over Penny. She wondered how Mrs. Gibson was going to respond to Penny reporting Courtney's indiscretions twice in two days. Maybe she should just go straight to the dean.

Penny made significant progress on her rough draft, put her work carefully away, and then went to the showers. The warm water rinsing off the soap lather from her body felt good. She thought about people like Courtney who relished sin in their life. It was hard to imagine not feeling dirty when engaged in lying, cheating, and defiant behavior. As she washed, Penny prayed and thanked God for the ability to be clean, inside and outside.

9

> "Give me a sign of your goodness, that my enemies may see it and be put to shame, for you, O Lord, have helped me and comforted me." Psalm 86:17

Penny woke up earlier than usual, got her shower and dressed. Grabbing her Bible, she went downstairs to the lobby and curled up on a couch, pulling an afghan over her lap. She began reading the Lord's prayer in Matthew and came to the verse, "forgive us our trespasses as we forgive those who trespass against us." Placing her hand on the page, Penny closed her eyes and reviewed her own sins.

There was the Sunday she lied to her uncle about an assignment so she could spend the afternoon with him. She felt so guilty that she didn't enjoy the day and ended up with a stomachache. There was also the time when she found a ring on the floor of the cafeteria and waited three days to turn it in so she could imagine it as hers for a while. When she did turn it in, she lied about when she found it.

Penny spent summers at her uncle's small apartment and loved their time together but remembered the jealousy she felt about the girls who were spending time with their families at lake homes or vacation spots around the world. Penny also recalled not speaking up in defense of one of the girls being gossiped about. No, Penny was not perfect but she was forgiven. She had confessed her sins and made amends when she could. Her sins now were only memories of God's grace.

Penny always had a strong sense of right and wrong that didn't let her do wrong for long or tolerate wrongdoing in others. As she got older, she had to balance this with the social relationships she enjoyed. Her thoughts turned to Courtney. Penny was not responsible for Courtney's sins nor was she the judge of them. But she did have an obligation under the Code of Ethics. Courtney's trespasses involved others and broke school rules.

"Oh, God, please help me find a way to help Courtney stay out of trouble," Penny whispered.

"What did you say?"

Penny opened her eyes and saw Courtney standing over her.

"Were you sleeping? Your eyes were closed and I thought you were talking in your sleep."

"No, Courtney. I was just praying." Penny swung her feet of the couch and patted the cushion next to her.

"Oh. I thought I heard my name."

"Probably. I pray for you everyday, Courtney. Have a seat and tell me what you are doing up so early."

"I wanted to talk to you about my paper. You made a suggestion last night that I've been thinking about. Do you really think Mrs. Belford would let me change my outline to include my family's personal connection to Eleanor Roosevelt?"

"I think she would, especially if you have documentation. You could tell her about it and ask her for permission to redo your outline. I'm sure it will be much more impressive after you rewrite it."

"Yea, I guess. I'd have to really scramble to do a new outline and finish the rough draft by next week."

"You can do it Courtney. Go see Mrs. Belford first thing and get it approved."

"I will. Thanks, Penny. You've really helped me. I'll let you get back to your reading or praying or whatever you are doing." Courtney smiled at her roommate, turned and went up the stairs.

Penny marveled at the first genuine smile Courtney ever gave her and the answer to a prayer uttered just a few moments before. If Courtney rewrote her outline, she would have to write her rough draft based on the new outline and end up turning in her own paper! She would not be guilty of turning in a paper bought from Kerry and Penny would not have to report her! Now Penny would have to pray that Mrs. Belford would permit Courtney changing her paper. But then, she imagined that God had already taken care of that when he brought about the entire conversation. God was so good! Penny wished she could tell Mrs. Gibson but decided she better keep this miracle to herself and see what God was going to do!

10

> "A little that a righteous man hath is better
> than the riches of many wicked."
> Psalm 37:16

The next few days passed quickly. Whatever was happening about Courtney's smoking was not evident to Penny. On Wednesday, the announcement was posted listing the candidates for student council officers. The candidates for recording secretary were as expected Penny and Courtney. The girls in the dorm quickly divided loyalties. Most of the long-time residents were supporting Penny. The newer residents were campaigning for Courtney. Because they were roommates, the two girls agreed not to bring the campaign into their room. Penny prayed the campaign would bring them closer, though it was hard to imagine how that would happen.

Julia and Mary Ann followed through on their promise to manage Penny's campaign. The three met after supper for a strategy meeting.

"Penny, Courtney really wants this job and will be fighting dirty. What can we use against her?" Julie asked.

"Use against her? Nothing! Julia, we will not say or do anything against Courtney. I'm serious about this. We will run a positive campaign or none at all."

"But," Mary Ann interjected, "Courtney is already saying things about you. She said you don't deserve the job because you aren't paying tuition."

Penny gasped.

"Is that what the girls care about?"

"Heavens, no! Nobody who really knows you cares how you are here, they are just glad you are!" Julia declared defiantly.

"Listen, I appreciate you wanting to protect me but we will not react to any attack. I want to run on a campaign of how I can serve the student body of this school. I will not speak of Courtney or criticize her in any way. If the girls choose her, so be it. God will work it all out for my good."

Julia and Mary Ann looked at each other. They knew Penny

meant every word she said. Their friend's frequent mention of God was not just pretty speech. Penny Wilburn was the real thing when it came to being a Christian. She walked her talk. They knew God would do his work but, as her flesh and blood friends, they would watch her back very closely.

On Thursday morning, Courtney's campaign was in full swing. At breakfast, pink balloon bouquets with "Courtney" in silver lettering decorated tables in the dorm dining rooms. Her posters were professionally printed with a color portrait of Courtney and "Courtney for Recording Secretary" on them. 45 records of "Bikini Beach" sung by Annette Funicello were on each table, each with a handwritten note from Courtney asking for the recipient's vote. Contrary to the glitter of Courtney's campaign, each of Penny's posters had a flattering caricature of Penny in a school uniform drawn by Julia. The name Penny was outlined with real pennies and the motto "Penny Makes Cents for Recording Secretary." Penny also had a giveaway, new and shiny pennies her uncle got for her at the bank. Penny visited all the dorms and spoke to each girl individually. She asked girls who were returning students how they were doing and reminisced with each one. Penny made a special point to introduce herself to each new girl, offering friendship and mentoring as each got settled at Charlotte Hills. She explained that she wanted to help their school be the very best and needed their vote to be recording secretary. Handing the girl a penny, she asked each to remember her when they voted.

Penny and Courtney kept their word about keeping the campaign out of their room. Penny focused on her studies and Courtney worked on a new outline and rough draft that included personal references about Eleanor Roosevelt. Penny was giddy about how God had answered her prayer.

The Student Council election was held on the third Tuesday of the term. On Monday afternoon, an election rally was held when each candidate would speak for one minute. The candidates for representatives for grades seven and above were heard from first and then the candidates for offices from the junior and senior class came next. Two girls spoke about the position of treasurer. Each had been at Charlotte Hills for several years and had been good friends of Penny. Next came the position of Recording Secretary.

Courtney was called first.

Courtney, her blond hair perfectly coiffed with pink and silver ribbons, strutted to the podium. She flashed a smile and waved seductively at the audience.

"Hello," Courtney began, "my name is Courtney Guilford. My father is U.S. Senator Martin Guilford. He has served North Carolina for eighteen years. I love politics. I want to be a politician when I grow up. I also like music and movies. Annette Funicello is my favorite from both. I hope each of you got the record I bought you."

A murmur of assent purred through the crowd. Courtney smiled and nodded.

"You are all welcome. I knew you would like it. Please think of me when you listen to it and especially when you vote.

"I am new to Charlotte Hills. It is the best school my parents could find and I am so glad I am here. Where I come from, we value education and are willing to pay a lot of money for the very best. My opponent has been here for eight years as an act of charity. She is my roommate and a very sweet girl. But my background, money, and experience make me the best candidate. Being recording secretary here at Charlotte Hills will be my first job and one that I will be very proud to have on my resume. Please vote for me."

Courtney glided back to her seat on the wave of applause that followed her speech. The dean called for Penny Wilburn to come forward. A hush filled the crowd. Julia murmured to Mary Ann, "For once in her life, I wish Penny would get mad and get even!"

Penny stepped swiftly to the podium. She only had one minute and wanted to make the most of her time. She began to speak confidently with a strong, modulated voice.

"I want to thank the administration of Charlotte Hills Academy for giving me and the others who are speaking today the opportunity to express how we want to serve this great school. Service is what we should all be about. I want to serve by helping my sister students each achieve her very best. I want to serve by supporting the faculty and administration in their efforts to continue making Charlotte Hills Academy a school of excellence. I want to serve those who love me by being everything that God

46

planned for me to be. Service should be what we are seeking, not power or political influence."

Penny continued to speak with conviction.

"I have loved and appreciated every moment I have been privileged to be a student here. I want to give back to this school in the position of recording secretary for the student council. I will be diligent in my responsibilities, meticulous in my duties, and always willing to do my best for this school. Thank you for your continued trust and your vote."

Penny returned to her seat while the crowd politely applauded. Speeches of the candidates for vice president and president followed. After the rally, each candidate was surrounded by their close friends and well wishers. Julia and Mary Ann got to Penny as quickly as they could.

"Oh, Penny, you were wonderful! Mary Ann gushed.

"Thanks, Mary Ann. What do you think, Julia?"

"I think Courtney is horrible! She thinks she is so hot but she is just, just HORRIBLE!"

"It's all right, Julia," Penny answered.

"Penny, are you going to give up?"

"No, I'm not giving up. But I will work within the system. The votes will be counted. If the majority vote for Courtney, then we will get what we vote for, someone who wants the position for power and not service. I hope that came across in my speech. Let's go to supper now. I'm really hungry. It's meatloaf tonight, right?"

The three girls went to the Bryant Hall dining room. Penny was greeted by several girls with "nice speech" and "good luck." As Penny got to the table with her tray, Courtney met her there.

"Penny, that was a great speech. It should be a good election. Good luck."

"Thanks, Courtney. If you will excuse me, I'm going to eat now."

Courtney stood there as if she was waiting for Penny to tell her how wonderful her speech was and return the well wishes. But Penny pulled out her chair and sat down, joined by Julia, Mary Ann, and several other girls.

"Well, I guess I'll go get my own supper, then." Courtney turned quickly and walked away.

"Was I bad, Julia?" Penny asked her friend with twinkling eyes.

"NO! She was wanting you to fawn all over her and you didn't give her the satisfaction. Proud of you, Penny."

The girls enjoyed their supper of meatloaf and mashed potatoes, green peas, carrot salad, and apple pie. On the other side of the dining room, Courtney's friends chattered excitedly while Courtney kept looking across the room at Penny. The determination to win the election and show her superiority to this little orphan girl everybody liked so much was stronger than ever. Penny would find out you can't run against a Guilford and win.

"Hey girls, did you know Mrs. Gibson has a boyfriend?"

11

> "Wealth and honor come from you; you are the ruler of all things. In your hands are strength and power to exalt and give strength to all. Now, our God, we give you thanks, and praise your glorious name."
> 1 Chronicles 29:12-13

By breakfast, Courtney's question had electrified the Bryant Hall residents. The long time residents loved Mrs. Gibson and were aghast that she was the subject of gossip. The newcomers were titillated in their imaginations. The dorm mother was an attractive woman in her mid thirties but gave no indication of involvement in anything but school and church activities and relationships. Was she really living a double life?

Penny was late getting to breakfast and assumed the tone of the room was due to the election. Julia and Mary Ann had finished eating but were waiting for Penny at their usual table.

"Hey, what's up?"

The two friends looked at each other and Julia nudged Mary Ann.

"Penny, there's some gossip going around."

"What are they saying about me now, Mary Ann?"

Julia jumped in.

"It's not about you, Penny."

"That's good. Then we shouldn't be talking about it should we."

Julia and Mary Ann looked at each other again. This time Mary Ann nudged Julia.

"Uh, Penny, it's about Mrs. Gibson. Do you want to know what they're saying?"

The color drained from Penny's face. What she wanted to do was go crawl into her bed and get out of the storm that suddenly swirled around her.

"What?"

"What I heard was that Mrs. Gibson was having an affair with somebody in administration. They say she went away with him

49

during the summer. Somebody even said they saw her making out with a man in the stables."

Penny stared at Julia.

"You're kidding! That is so ridiculous."

"Yea," Julia quipped. "Who would believe such a thing?"

Penny looked across the cafeteria, her eyes searching out Courtney. At that moment, Courtney, laughing with her friends, looked over at Penny, their eyes locking.

Penny got a sick feeling in her stomach. Not only would Courtney believe such a lie, she easily could have started it.

"I've got to go," Penny said quietly. She picked up her tray of untouched food, dropped it at the kitchen window and hurried toward the exit. Several girls stopped her and told her good luck with the election. She thanked them with a smile that was forced. This was not who she was. Penny dashed to the nearest restroom, closed herself into a stall and bent over a toilet, throwing up a breakfast she hadn't eaten.

#####

Voting was conducted during first period classes. Ballots were marked and turned in to teachers who put them in an envelope and sealed it. Mrs. Tucker picked up all the envelopes and took them back to Dean Derrick's office.

Dean Merrick was troubled by the candidacy of Courtney Guilford. Rebecca Gibson had been told that a reprimand had been placed in Courtney's file. That was true but it was actually just a notation of "unsubstantiated accusation regarding the infraction of school rule 24b."

Several more notations could have been made to the file but President Garvin was ever mindful of the benevolence of the Guilford family to Charlotte Hills Academy and had ordered Dean Merrick to bury both the smoking incident and any other negative issues regarding Courtney Guilford.

To have Courtney on the student council was unconscionable and Dean Merrick hoped she would not have the votes. He could override the ballots but he would be risking his own security by manipulating the election. Maybe, just maybe, Penny would win outright.

Both the dean and his secretary, Mrs. Tucker opened and counted the ballots. It was a close election in all the races. After counting the Guilford-Wilburn votes, Dean Merrick asked Mrs. Tucker to get the school president on the phone.

"President Garvin, I wanted to tell you that we have elected the student council. Yes, sir, she did. Well, we will have to see. I hope not. Yes, sir. I know. The results will be posted at closing bell today."

The closer it got to the 3 o'clock bell, the more anxious the students got. They knew that the student council results would be announced. The race that everybody cared most about was the one between Penny and Courtney.

Penny dawdled in the classroom after closing bell. Since breakfast, she had avoided personal contact with anyone. The crowd rushing to the bulletin board outside the dean's office was especially not something she wanted to be part of. She would hear soon enough.

Penny walked down the deserted hallway toward the stairs. Suddenly Julia and Mary Ann came around the corner and almost knocked her down.

"Penny, there you are! You won! You beat Courtney!"

Penny's started expression grew to a smile.

"I did? Does Courtney know?"

"Yea, she was there. She was really mad and said some bad words. I'd stay away from her if I was you," Mary Ann answered.

"That's not going to be easy since we are roommates! Come on, let's go to the library. I have to turn in my books on Helen Keller before they are late."

The next two hours passed quickly. As the trio walked to the library, they encountered several girls who congratulated Penny on her election. They also saw other girls who turned away quickly without remark. Penny turned in the library books and the girls went to the fiction section to see what Grace Livingston Hill titles they had not read yet. Penny had already talked with Mrs. Gibson who agreed to be the GLH book club sponsor and make available the books she had in her personal collection.

"Look, here's one I want to read. It's about a girl who is orphaned and goes to live with her uncle. Isn't that something?"

"Could be your story, Penny."

"I like the stories about people during the depression. Makes me appreciate the blessings we have today," Julia commented.

All three girls checked a book out just before the library closed at 5 o'clock and went straight to the Bryant Hall dining room. Courtney was sitting at a table in the middle of the room surrounded by her clique. The room became silent when Penny got in the serving line. The three took their trays to a table that had empty seats. As Penny put her tray down, she turned in response to a tap on her shoulder.

Courtney had come up behind her, the eyes of everyone in the room watching each step with bated breath.

"Hello, Penny. Congratulations on winning the election." Courtney said quietly.

Penny replied quickly. "Thank you, Courtney. I appreciate you saying that."

"Uh huh. Well, I'll see you back in the room. Bye." Courtney answered and walked back to her seat. The room was suddenly filled with loud murmuring.

"Well, that's something I didn't expect to hear," Julia announced.

"Me, either," said Mary Ann.

"Courtney's o.k. We'll get past this."

"Penny, what about Mrs. Gibson?"

"Nothing to say or do. Uncle Bear told me once the best way to live is in such a way that when people speak evil against you, no one will believe it. I know Mrs. Gibson. You know her, too. She is a wonderful, honorable woman. Someone is trying to defame her.

God will avenge. I am really hungry. I'll say the blessing." The three girls clasped hands with each other and Penny offered thanks.

"Thank You, Heavenly Father, for this food we receive as nourishment for our bodies. We thank You for all your blessings, especially for the opportunity to serve this school and You in the position I have been elected to. Lord, I ask you to especially bless Mrs. Gibson and show her enemies the truth of who she truly is. And, dear Jesus, help Courtney to see me as a friend who cares about her. Amen."

Julia and Mary Ann looked at each other and rolled their eyes. Penny was in denial about Courtney. They would have to keep watching her back!

12

Penny stopped at Mrs. Gibson's room after supper.

"Hi, Penny. Congratulations on your election."

"Thanks. Are you doing o.k.?"

"I'm fine, Penny. Are you asking about the rumors?"

Penny looked down at the floor and bit her lip. A tear broke from her eye and crawled down her cheek.

"Penny, everything is fine. There is no relationship in my life that remotely resembles the gossip going around."

Penny smiled.

"I know. Does Uncle Bear know about this?"

"Come in, Penny. Let's sit and talk."

Penny went into the small apartment and sat on the couch. Mrs. Gibson took a seat beside her.

"Penny, when I met your uncle, I was a young widow who only wanted to find fulfillment in service here at Charlotte Hills. In these eight years, your uncle and I have become good friends. I will be honest with you and admit there is an emotional closeness that is growing between us but I want to assure you that our relationship is honorable. Your uncle heard the gossip and came to comfort me. We all know the truth and the truth will prevail."

Penny smiled.

"Thank you for being honest with me. Of course none of this is a surprise to me and I think you and Uncle Bear together are wonderful."

"Now, Penny. Let's not get ahead of ourselves."

The two laughed.

"Mrs. Gibson, I want to go see Uncle Bear and tell him about the election."

"That's fine, Penny. Enjoy your visit."

Penny briskly walked toward the administration building. Her uncle was sweeping fallen leaves from the basement stairwell and called to her.

"There she is, the new recording secretary of the student council!"

"You heard!"

"I sure did. I knew you would come. Let's go inside."

The two spent the next hour talking about the election while sharing a large piece of cake and two cartons of milk Baron had requisitioned from the kitchen. He was especially concerned about Courtney's response.

"She's already congratulated me. I think it will be all right."

"I hope so."

"Penny, I am so proud of you. I wish Helen was here to see what a beautiful and sweet young woman you have become."

Penny bit her lip to try to thwart the tears.

"I feel her watching me, Uncle Bear. She was so wonderful to me."

"And a wonderful wife to me. I regret I was not the husband I should have been. But we will both see her again, won't we?"

"Yes, sir."

"Penny, in the meantime, Rebecca Gibson is there for you. I know she has already helped you through a lot of your growing up. If you have any girl stuff to talk about, well..." Baron spoke clumsily.

"I know, Uncle Bear. She is wonderful, isn't she? I'm good right now. I promise not to grow up too fast."

Baron grinned and grabbed Penny in a hug. The two said goodnight and Baron watched Penny walk back to Bryant Hall. Seeing her climb the steps and entering the front door, he turned toward his room with a prayer that God would protect her from anything or anyone that would hurt her, including Courtney Guilford.

As Penny entered the foyer of Bryant Hall, she recognized the blond hair of Courtney pass through the door that led to the basement. *Now what is she up to?* Penny wondered as she stepped toward the door her roommate had just entered and quietly opened it, peering down the stairs. A muffled giggle floated from the dark abyss.

"Courtney, are you down there," Penny called from the top of the stairs.

A silence enveloped the obscurity and a sound of footsteps rose toward where Penny stood in the open doorway. Suddenly, Courtney appeared from the dark.

"Geez, Penny. Are you following me?" Courtney demanded as she shut the basement door behind her.

"No. I saw you go into the basement and wanted to make sure you were all right. The lighting is not very good down there."

"Well, I'm fine. Just putting a box of election stuff away. Not that it is any of your business. And I have a light," Courtney responded angrily, holding up a flashlight. She stomped up the stairs to the second floor dorm rooms, leaving Penny standing by herself. Penny looked back at the basement door and started to open it again and take another look. But a sudden shudder of fear stopped her. Whatever or whoever was in that basement was not something she needed to investigate. Penny went down the hall to Mrs. Gibson's room. She didn't want to tattle on Courtney again but thought she should report something.

"Hello Penny. Did you and your uncle enjoy your visit?" Rebecca Gibson asked when she saw Penny standing outside her door for the second time that evening.

"Yes, ma'am, we did. Um, I just came in and heard a noise from the basement. Do you think somebody should check it out?"

The dorm mother suddenly looked concerned. "A noise? What kind of a noise?"

Penny spoke carefully. "I don't know. I opened the door but it is so dark down there. It could have been voices."

Mrs. Gibson went to her room phone and called security. Within five minutes, two campus officers went down the basement steps with bright searchlights. In a short time, they came back into the building through the front door. One of the officers gave their report.

"You were right, Mrs. Gibson. It looks like somebody entered the basement through the cellar and had set up a little party down there. Found some beer bottles, blanket and pillows, and candles. We'll request maintenance to put a key lock on both the cellar door and this door so the little lovebirds can't get back to their nest."

Mrs. Gibson looked at Penny. "Is there anything else you

remember?"

Penny suddenly yawned. "I am really tired, Mrs. Gibson. It's really a mystery, isn't it? I'm going on to bed. Goodnight." Penny hurried away from the scene. She knew Mrs. Gibson could tell if she tried to lie and she did not want to involve Courtney in any more trouble.

Penny stopped in the bathroom before going to her room. As she looked in the mirror, she saw guilt. She had not lied but she was deceptive. A tear fell from her eye. Wiping it away, Penny knew she would have to repent of her deception. Or would she? Maybe if Courtney admitted being in the basement, she would not have to tattle, again. Courtney was already in bed when Penny got to the room. She changed into her nightclothes and got into her own bed. What the officer said troubled her. Evidently Courtney was meeting someone in the basement, a boy who entered Bryant Hall through the cellar door. No wonder Courtney was so mad when she came up those stairs. Penny had interrupted a secret liaison. Was there no end to Courtney's transgressions?

Penny huddled beneath her quilt and fingered the fabric she loved. In the eight years since the tornado, God had taken her through so much. She knew she was loved. She was blessed with a wonderful place to live and go to school. She had countless friends, evidently more than she had thought since she actually won the election against Courtney. There was the prospect of romance for Uncle Bear and Mrs. Gibson. Her life would be perfect if it weren't for all the drama Courtney involved her in.

"Dear Lord, I'm sorry I didn't tell the whole truth. You have kept me safe through all the storms so far. Help me to continue to trust you. And, Lord, help me to love Courtney! Amen."

13

> "Hatred stirs up dissension, but love covers over all wrongs."
> Proverbs 10:12

Wednesday morning, Penny woke early and slipped out of the room to do her devotions. When she returned, Courtney had dressed and was brushing her hair.

"Good morning, Courtney. Did you sleep well?"

Courtney said nothing. She threw the brush down on her vanity, pulled her books together and walked out of the room.

OK, I get the silent treatment. After making her bed and tidying her part of the room, Penny dressed and got her own books and went to the dining hall. The fire about Mrs. Gibson seemed to have died for lack of fuel, as Penny expected. With the election over and lost, Courtney found a way to keep the attention on her by talking incessantly about her 16th birthday that weekend. She was being picked up Friday at noon by a limo and taken home for a big party Saturday night. Courtney wanted to have a party at school but since dorm rules prohibited any private parties on campus, the Thursday night supper turned into a mini birthday celebration. A cake, ordered by Courtney's mother, was delivered from a local bakery. Mrs. Gibson approved music during dinner and the sounds of Annette Funicello filled the dining hall.

Penny enjoyed the festivity with the rest of the girls. Courtney was still not speaking to her but had kept her anger toward Penny private and worked hard to avoid any opportunity that put her in a position to have to speak to Penny. As far as the other girls knew, Penny and Courtney, while not friends, were not unfriendly.

Penny looked forward to the weekend. Courtney would be gone. The first meeting of the Grace Livingston Hill Reading Club was Friday afternoon in Mrs. Gibson's apartment right after closing bell. While the other girls went home for the weekend, she would spend her Saturday curled up with a good book. Then there was Sunday. The prospect of spending the day with Uncle Bear and Mrs. Gibson at church and dinner made her very happy.

The closeness between Uncle Bear and Mrs. Gibson was on

Penny's mind. For the first time in eight years, she felt hopeful that she would once again have a real home with two parents. Maybe this weekend she would have an opportunity to talk with her uncle about his intentions!

Friday morning, Penny placed a homemade birthday card on Courtney's vanity and left the room while Courtney was in the shower. She and the other student council members had a breakfast meeting with the dean in the administration's conference room. The meeting was to orient the elected members in their new positions. The dean was helpful and encouraged the members to work together to make the 1964-65 school year the best ever.

Following the meeting, Dean Warrick came up to Penny as she gathered her books to go to class.

"How are you, Miss Wilburn?"

"I'm fine, thank you, sir."

"It is unfortunate that you and Courtney Guilford had to run against each other. I hope it hasn't been too uncomfortable for you, being roommates and all," the dean remarked apologetically.

"Oh, we're getting along pretty well. We're two very different people and it'll take a while to be good friends."

"And losing the election? How did Miss Guilford react?"

"We've put it behind us. Thank you for your concern, Dean. And thank you for this wonderful breakfast. I hope I don't disappoint you as recording secretary."

"I'm sure you won't. You take care now, Penny."

Dean Warrick moved on to say goodbye to the other students. Penny went to her history class. When she got there, Courtney was already holding court. When Courtney saw Penny, she turned her back toward her. Mrs. Belford finally got the girls to take their seats.

"Class, I am returning your outlines. Hopefully they won't dampen your weekend."

She picked up a set of papers from her desk and continued: "On a whole, they are pretty good. Some of you have a lot of work to bring your paper into compliance with the format I gave you before you started. I want you to spend the rest of this period reviewing these papers and working on your rough draft which is due next Wednesday."

Mrs. Belford handed out the papers to many gasps and some groans. Penny, sitting across the room, watched Courtney receive her paper and quietly read it. Penny hoped Courtney's decision to rewrite her outline and not buy her paper from Kerry Andrews had proved favorable.

Penny was handed her own paper and was delighted to see only favorable comments throughout the text and a 100% at the top. It would be easy to do the rough and final draft from this outline. Looking up, Penny saw Courtney at Mrs. Belford's desk. Their intense conversation made Penny nervous. Then Courtney took her seat and pulled out a piece of notebook paper and started writing. Penny went back to her own paper and was engrossed in writing her introduction when she heard the bell ring and sensed someone standing in front of her. Looking up, she saw Courtney.

"Hi, Courtney," Penny said softly.

"Here, this is for you." Courtney replied nervously as she handed a folded sheet of paper to Penny, then turned and left the room.

Penny stared at the paper. What could this be about, she wondered. The next group of students were coming into the classroom so Penny stuck the paper in her notebook and hurried to her next class. Settling into her seat, she pulled the paper out of the notebook with trepidation.

Recognizing Courtney's exquisite handwriting, Penny read:

Dear Penny,

I want you to know Mrs. Belford really liked my paper and gave me a 100% on my new outline. I told her you had encouraged me to make the changes in my outline and she said I should thank you. Getting this grade really makes me happy and I do want to thank you for your help.

I have been angry with you about the election and am sorry for my attitude. You will make a wonderful recording secretary. You have only been kind to me and I have not appreciated you. I promise to be nicer to you when I get back. We'll talk then.
Courtney

Penny was delightfully surprised at the letter. Looking up, she saw Courtney enter the room. When their eyes met, Courtney had a smile on her face. Penny smiled back. As the class was called to order, Penny said a quick prayer, thanking God for this miracle. For the first time, Penny looked forward to the end of the weekend and Courtney's return to campus.

14

> "Godliness with contentment is great gain."
> 1 Timothy 6:6

Penny was engrossed with *Spice Box*, a GLH book Julia had read and recommended. Just before noon, Rebecca Gibson came to Penny's room and knocked on the open door.

"Hi, Penny. What are you working on?" Rebecca asked.

"I should be working on my history paper but can't put this book down."

"Your uncle called me and asked if the two of us would like to go to town with him. He has to pick up some supplies and thought we would like to ride along and maybe get some burgers."

"You bet." Penny adjusted her bookmark and placed the book on her desk. "Spending time with the two of you trumps reading a good book."

Penny and Rebecca walked down the stairs and out the front door of Bryant Hall to see Penny's Uncle Baron standing by his car. Penny ran to him and hugged him hard.

"Oh, Uncle Bear, this will be so much fun!"

The three climbed in the car, Penny sitting between Baron and Rebecca. On the way to town, Penny filled them in about Courtney's letter and how hopeful she was that she and her roommate were finally going to get along.

"Penny, I surely hope you and Courtney can be friends, now," answered Rebecca softly. "I would still be cautious, though."

Baron spoke in harsher tones: "Rebecca is being too careful with her words. You watch your back, Penny. I don't trust her. She is a very spoiled girl."

"I'll be fine, Uncle Bear. With my schoolwork and now my responsibilities on the student council, I shouldn't have too much contact with her outside our room. If we can get along there, we should not have any problems."

Changing the subject, Baron asked Rebecca about the basement intruder.

"Any idea who was down there?"

"I think one of the girls was planning on entertaining a boy from the outside," she answered.

"That's not going to happen anymore. Our staff has put locks on all the cellar doors so no one can get into any of the buildings through them."

"I'm wondering which of the girls was involved? Any ideas, Penny?"

"I wouldn't put it past the Guilford girl," Baron interjected.

"Courtney? She…"

Suddenly a dog ran into the road and Baron swerved to miss him, taking everyone's mind off Courtney and leaving Penny wondering what she was about to say.

The dog avoided and no one more than a bit disheveled, the conversation turned to the upcoming revival meeting at the church. Mrs. Gibson said that the school had gotten permission from the parents and would allow the girls to go to the evening services as long as their schoolwork did not suffer. Each girl had to get her teachers to sign off on the evening excursions.

"I'm going to try to get Courtney to go on youth night," Penny announced.

"That would be a coup d'état," Mrs. Gibson replied.

"A what?" Baron laughed.

"It's French, Uncle Bear. It means stroke of state. In other words, church is the last place Mrs. Gibson expects to see Courtney!"

Baron laughed. "I think I have two fancy talking girls with me. Where do you smart ladies want to have lunch?" Baron answered.

Penny saw a Burger King ahead and suggested they eat there. Baron pulled into the parking lot and the three went in to enjoy a leisurely Saturday lunch. Penny and Rebecca chose regular burgers while Baron got a whopper to eat with their fries and cokes. Grasping hands, Baron thanked the Lord for their food and time together and asked for God to give them guidance about their future. The guidance about their future part caused Penny to wonder but she was immediately drawn into the enjoyment of their special lunch.

"This whopper sure is big. You girls have to get one next time. Worth every bit of 89 cents." Baron exclaimed.

"Too much sandwich for me," Rebecca quipped.

"Me, too," added Penny.

Baron finished his sandwich and leaned back on the vinyl covered booth seat. As he looked across the table at Penny and Rebecca, he thought about how much God had blessed him in his life. He and Helen had a good marriage that he didn't appreciate until she was gone. Penny was the joy of his life, as if she were his own daughter. His work was satisfying and providing his and Penny's needs. To top everything, Rebecca had come into his life. He noticed her warmth and sincerity the first time he met her. Her devotion to the Lord and her work with the girls at Charlotte Hills was inspiring. Finally, Rebecca's love and protective attitude for Penny was what put him over the top. Baron Sanford was in love. His life as a farmer turned janitor provided for Penny and him, but how could he give Rebecca the kind of life and home she deserved?

Rebecca looked up from her meal at Baron. God had brought this wonderful man and child into her life. She admired his devotion to Penny and his willingness to take pride in a job that many would think was beneath their dignity. But Baron Sanford was a man of dignity and respect, a man she had come to cherish and love. She knew what he meant in his prayer. It was a yet unspoken understanding between the two that their separate lives were moving toward one at some point in the future as God led.

The three finished their lunch and got back in the car. Baron drove to Scotties Hardware and went inside, leaving Rebecca and Penny in the car alone.

Sitting beside Mrs. Gibson, Penny felt an overwhelming sense of contentment at that moment. She thought about Courtney who was probably right now getting primped and ready for her birthday party. Courtney had nothing in her life Penny envied. Penny had turned sixteen earlier in the summer but no party she could have had could give her the joy she felt in her heart at that moment sitting there with Mrs. Gibson and watching for Uncle Bear to come and sit on the other side of her.

Baron came out of the store and put a box in the back seat of the car. Sliding into the driver's seat, he immediately turned the radio on, his face registering concern.

"I heard inside that a line of severe weather is coming toward us from the west. We need to get back to the school as soon as we can to avoid driving in the storm."

As they listened to the warnings on the radio, Rebecca reached over and took Penny's hand.

"It will be all right, Penny. We'll get home before it starts, won't we Baron."

"Lord willing and the creek don't rise!" he quipped, trying to lighten Penny's mood.

Driving toward a storm was something Penny never dreamed she would have to do. It was not yet 2 o'clock in the afternoon and the sky was a greenish gray instead of the bright blue they enjoyed just an hour ago. On the horizon was a line of black that appeared to stretch upward as they drove toward it. The leaves on the trees were beginning to whip around. Baron gripped the steering wheel and drove as quickly as he could to cover the twenty miles to Charlotte Hills Academy. As they pulled into the gate, the first drops of water fell unto the windshield. Baron drove the women to Bryant Hall and stopped the car.

"You two get inside as quick as you can. Rebecca, you'll stay with her for awhile?" Baron asked.

Penny got out of the car and ran up the steps. Rebecca paused long enough to say goodbye.

"Don't worry about her, Baron. I'll stay as long as I need to. I love her, too."

"I know. Thanks. See you later."

Rebecca followed Penny to the second floor. Penny was in the

65

bed, gripping her quilt. The confidence she exhibited just an hour ago had dissolved to panic that intensified with every sound of thunder and bolt of lightning. Rebecca sat on the bed and rubbed Penny's back. Softly she started singing.

"God will take care of you, through every day, o'er all the way, He will take care of you, God will take care of you."

Penny peaked out from under her quilt.

"Aunt Helen sang that to me when I was little."

"Did she?"

"Uh, huh."

"It's a special promise. No matter what happens, God is still in control."

"I know. He was taking care of me even in the tornado. He protected me and Uncle Bear so we could be saved. We would not be here and know you if the tornado had not happened. I don't understand God's ways but I trust Him. I just don't like storms!"

Mrs. Gibson chuckled.

"Nobody blames you for that, Penny. But at the end of every storm is the sign of his promise, a rainbow. That's what we look for."

Penny sat up and the two chatted about the book club. Mrs. Gibson reminisced about the Grace Livingston Hill books she read as a teenage girl.

"I loved to read and the house parents had only Christian fiction available at the home, mostly Grace Livingston Hill. I read one after another and they helped form my values. I knew I wanted to marry a godly man who loved the Lord with all his heart. I also wanted a home that honored God and children who we would rear in the nurture and admonition of the Lord."

Rebecca Gibson sighed and looked away.

"I'm sorry, Mrs. Gibson. You would have made a wonderful mother. You are a wonderful mother to me!"

Mrs. Gibson stroked Penny's hair and smiled.

"What about you, Penny. Have you begun thinking about the kind of life you want to have as an adult?"

Penny thought back to the stumbling comments of her uncle. "Have you and Uncle Bear been talking about me?" She asked with a grin.

"Well, you are sixteen. You are a smart girl and it's time you start planning on college. As for dating, there's plenty of time for that. You are a pretty girl and I know there are some boys at church that like you. One asked me recently if you are allowed to date."

"Really?"

"Yes, really!"

Penny blushed.

"What did you tell him?"

"I pointed to your uncle and said he had to ask Mr. Sanford's permission to take you out."

"That will scare him away!"

"I think it did."

"As for college, I'd like to go to a Christian school, study education, and be a teacher. I'm working hard and hoping to get some scholarships. As for life in general, I do want the same as you said, to marry a man who loves the Lord and me for who I am."

"God will honor those desires, Penny. I'm believing that with you. Feel better?"

"Yes."

"Good. Oh, look, the sun is shining."

Mrs. Gibson went to the window and pulled back the curtain.

"Come look, Penny."

The two gazed toward the southwestern sky just over the tree line. There was a rainbow, not an ordinary rainbow but a double one!

"Look, Penny, there's one for each of us."

15

Courtney was holding court in the dining hall when Penny went down to supper Sunday evening, the girls buzzing around her like bees on a honeycomb. She regaled the swarm with stories about her birthday weekend. Penny avoided the crowd and went to the far corner of the room where Julia joined her.

"What's going on with Courtney?" Penny asked.

"Oh, she's talking about some boy she met at her party. According to her he's the most handsome, rich, and sweetest guy she has ever known."

"Courtney is boy crazy. All she ever talks about in our room is Annette Funicello and boys!"

"Yea, wait till you see her hair. She said it was just like Annette's on her latest album cover."

Julia looked around, leaned over to Penny, and whispered, "Courtney's not the only one who met a boy this weekend!"

Penny dropped her jaw and mocked, "She wasn't!"

Julia giggled. "No, I met someone, too. His name is Tim and he is a senior at James Madison High School in town."

"When and where did you meet him?"

"At the movies, Friday night. He was one of the ushers at the Cineplex. I was standing in line for popcorn and we got to talking. He asked me for my number."

"And you said, no!" Penny responded jokingly.

"And I said, yes!" Julia responded, punching her friend lightly in the arm.

"Did he call?"

"Yea, Saturday. He took me to the Cineplex Saturday night. He gets free admission. We saw *Mary Poppins*."

""I've heard about that movie. Was it good?"

"Oh, yes. A lot of fun to see. It's about..."

"Don't tell me! Maybe I'll get to see it one day."

"Not if you don't get out away from this school sometimes. Why don't you come home with me one weekend? Jim can get one of his buddies and we can double date."

"I'm sure that would be fun but I don't think Uncle Bear is ready for me to date yet."

"Have you talked to him about it?"

"Well, no. Mrs. Gibson and I talked about stuff like that a little this weekend. She and Uncle Bear are double teaming me about growing up. I think there are some other things going on between them, too. She has been joining us for more and more of our outings."

"Really? Wow, isn't that something. Do you think they like each other that way?"

"I think so. Wouldn't that be wonderful, Julia."

"What would be wonderful?"

The girls looked up to see Courtney standing in front of them.

Julia grabbed a napkin, choking on a meatball she had just put in her mouth."

"Hi, Courtney. Was your party everything you expected it to be?" Penny responded.

"Oh, yes! What would be wonderful?" Courtney persisted.

Penny did not want to talk about her uncle and Mrs. Gibson to Courtney and quickly changed the subject.

"I think it would be wonderful if you and the other girls from Bryant would all come to the revival service at my church next week."

"Church? That may be wonderful for you but sounds like torture to me. I thought you were talking about something fun."

"Penny's church is fun, Courtney. I went with her one weekend when I stayed on campus and had a great time!" Julia retorted.

Penny said nothing. She didn't want to start off their newfound friendship by telling Courtney just how insulting what she said was. Again, she changed the subject.

"So, tell us about your party."

"Oh, it was great! Guess who was there? Oh, you would never guess, I'll just tell you! Annette Funicello was there and sang all my favorite songs! I danced with her, too! See my hair? It matches her new album that just came out. She autographed it for me!"

"Wow, Courtney! Did you know she was coming?" Julia asked.

"No way! Daddy got her as a surprise for me. He paid her $10,000 personal appearance fee and all her expenses to come. He's the greatest dad!"

"And," Courtney continued, "I met the most handsome guy. His name is Ken and we danced all night. When Annette left, we walked her to the limo and on the way back, slipped to the side of the house and made out. He is such a good kisser!"

Julia giggled and Penny cast her eyes downward.

"There you are, Penny the prude! There is nothing wrong with making out! We didn't go all the way. Just some necking and petting. See my hickey?" Courtney pulled her sweater away from her neck and giggled.

Penny hated the lingo her roommate was using and was certain she didn't want to get any lessons on love and dating from Courtney.

"I have to go. I want to speak to Mrs. Belford before history class starts. See you girls later."

Penny grabbed her tray and headed to the tray return window. After disposing of her dishes, she went up to her room, got her books for the day, and went to the classroom building. As she walked, she remembered her prayer of that morning when she asked God to help her be a witness for Jesus to Courtney. But how would she do that when Courtney had returned with such worldly experiences?

With the semester well under way, most of the girls spent their evenings doing homework or reading in their rooms. Penny had the extra duties of student council that met one afternoon a week. Courtney brought a collection of movie star magazines back to campus each Sunday night and spent her evening hours primping herself to match the looks she found in the celebrity pictures.

Friday afternoon, Penny walked in on Courtney packing her make-up case.

"Thought you had everything at home and didn't like packing for your home weekends," Penny commented.

"I do but I've been working all week on the look I want for

my date with Ken tomorrow night so I'm taking my make-up with me this trip."

"Where are you and Ken going?"

"He said he wanted to surprise me. Isn't that romantic."

"Courtney, are you sure about him? Do you know anything about his family?"

"Well, no. His cousin was one of the valets and told Ken about the party. Ken kind of crashed it. Isn't that the cutest!"

"Do your parents know he crashed the party?"

"Of course not. Why would I tell them that? What they don't know won't matter."

Penny shook her head and gathered the dirty clothes from the hamper and took them to the laundry chute. When she returned, Courtney was headed toward the stairs to meet her limo.

"Tootaloo," Courtney called to Penny.

"Take care," Penny responded as she watched Courtney disappear down the staircase.

16

> "He whose walk is blameless is kept safe,
> but he whose ways are perverse will suddenly fall."
> Proverbs 28:18

Revival services started at Grace Community Church on Sunday. All six girls who stayed at Bryant Hall that weekend went with Penny to the morning service and stayed afterward to enjoy the potluck dinner. Penny invited them to go back to the evening service and all six delighted her by showing up at the appointed time. Baron hadn't made arrangements to take the bus at night so all the girls tried to pile into the Sanford car until Mrs. Gibson drove up and took some of the girls with her. As they drove out the gate, Penny noticed the limo that brought Courtney back to school. If it had gotten back just thirty minutes before, perhaps she could have convinced Courtney to go to the service with them.

The girls got back to Bryant Hall a little after 9 p.m. and were urged to quickly get ready for lights out at 10 o'clock. Penny went to her room and was surprised that her roommate was not there. Courtney was still not back by ten and Penny went on to bed. As she lay there, she recounted the wonderful day at church. The music and messages had been so inspiring. Two of the girls had spoken to counselors during the invitation that evening and Penny hoped that they had been saved. She would speak with each tomorrow and tell them how wonderful being a Christian is. Before she drifted off to sleep, Penny asked God to watch over Courtney wherever she was.

As she was accustomed, Penny woke before the morning wake-up bell. Looking across the room, she was alarmed that Courtney was not there and her bed had not been disturbed. Penny quickly got into her clothes and opened the door to find her uncle, Mrs. Gibson, and two men in black suits about to knock.

Baron stepped quickly into the room and put his arm around Penny. She hugged him back.

"Uncle Bear! What are you doing here? Is something wrong?"

Rebecca Gibson spoke first.

"Penny, is Courtney here?"

"No, she did not come in last night. I just woke up and was coming to tell you. Do you know where she is?"

"Let's go inside your room, Penny," Mrs. Gibson said quietly as Penny backed up and the dorm mother and men entered the room and closed the door.

"What's wrong? Is Courtney all right?"

"We don't know, Penny. Sit down on your bed and listen to me. At 4 o'clock this morning, Courtney's mother got a phone call from someone who said they have Courtney and want money before they give her back. These men are from the FBI and want to talk to you. Just tell them what you know."

Tears suddenly came to her eyes as she realized the implications of what Mrs. Gibson described. Penny looked at her uncle who still had his arm around her shoulder.

"Yes, ma'am," she answered in a shaky voice.

The taller of the two men spoke first.

"Penny, I'm Agent Copeland with the FBI. Can you tell me what time you came to your room last night."

"It was a little after 9 o'clock."

"Why were you out so late?"

"I had gone to revival service at my church. A lot of the girls went."

"Did you see Courtney last night."

"Yes, well, I think I did. The car that brings her to school each Sunday night came through the gate as my uncle's car drove out. I saw someone with blond hair like Courtney's in the backseat."

"What time was that?"

Mrs. Gibson interjected, "I can answer that. I was right behind Mr. Sanford's car with some of the girls riding with me. We left at 6:15. I saw the same car and thought it strange that Courtney was getting back after supper which is served from 5 to 6 o'clock."

The second FBI agent stood by the window writing on a notepad while Agent Copeland continued to ask questions.

"Penny, when you came in the room last night, did it appear that Courtney had been here? Was it different from how you left it when you went to church?"

Penny thought back to the previous afternoon as she looked

around the room. Courtney's desk looked the same and so did her bed. Penny got up and went to the clothes hamper. Opening it, she stepped back in surprise.

"Friday afternoon, I emptied this into the laundry chute. Now it has one of Courtney's blouses in it." Penny started to reach in when Agent Copeland grabbed her arm.

"No, don't touch that." He took out a handkerchief from his breast pocket and used it to pull the blouse out of the hamper. The second man produced a plastic bag and the blouse was dropped in it.

"Penny you have helped us a great deal. We now know Courtney was here after 6:15 and changed her blouse. At 9 o'clock she was not here. Do you have any idea where she might have gone?"

Penny bit her lip. Her mind went back to the night she saw Courtney coming out of the basement.

"Have you looked in the basement? She keeps some stuff down there."

Mrs. Gipson shot a questioning look at Penny who blushed, blinked and lowered her eyes for a split second.

The men nodded to each other and the second man left the room quickly. "One more thing, Penny. Do you know if Courtney had a boyfriend?"

"Her birthday was last weekend and she met a boy named Ken at her party. She talked about him all week and said they were going to go out this weekend. Ken crashed her party. His cousin was one of the valets."

"Really? That's very interesting. Thank you, Penny. Mrs. Gibson, we appreciate your help, as well. We need you to call a meeting of all the girls in the building while we search their rooms."

"Yes, sir. The dean has already told me to hold all the girls at breakfast until he can meet with them."

"Well, then, we are done, here. Mr. Sanborn, thank you, sir."

The agent left the room and Mrs. Gibson closed the door behind him. When she turned around, she found Penny sobbing in her uncle's arms.

Rebecca Gibson stepped toward Penny. She looked into

Baron's troubled eyes and understood the helplessness he felt.

Putting her hand on Penny's shoulder, she pulled words from her heart.

"Penny. We have to trust God through this time. Nothing is happening that God does not already know about."

"But Courtney doesn't believe in God!"

"I know but He believes in her and loves her. God brought her here and has been working in her life to show her His love. Let's kneel at Courtney's bed right now and pray."

The three got on their knees on the side of Courtney's bed and prayed. Penny spoke first.

"Dear Jesus, Courtney..." Penny's voice erupted into a sob and Mrs. Gibson picked up the prayer.

"Lord, protect Courtney and bring her back to us. Show her your love and protection. We claim a miracle in Your name, Jesus."

Baron completed the brief prayer time, asking God to keep Courtney safe and help the authorities to find her and bring her home. They then walked through the hall and made sure all the girls knew to go to the dining hall. When they got to the dining room, most of the girls were already there wondering what was going on. Dean Warrick and President Garvin came in and called the girls to order.

"Are all the girls accounted for Mrs. Gibson?" Dean Warrick asked.

Mrs. Gibson looked around and nodded her head at the question.

"Mrs. Gibson," Mary Ann interrupted. "Courtney is not here."

"Yes, I know, Mary Ann."

In a clear, matter of fact voice, Dean Warrick spoke. "Girls, last evening Courtney Guilford returned to campus at approximately 6:15. Sometime between then and 9 o'clock, she disappeared. The FBI is on campus and is searching all the rooms in Bryant Hall. They have already searched the classroom building. When I dismiss you, please go directly to your first period classroom. If you saw Courtney last night or know anything about her plans or where she might be, please come directly to me or President Garvin now. You are dismissed."

A shuffling of chairs joined the hum of whispers for the next few moments. The girls moved quickly across the quadrangle to the classroom building. The school administrators were disappointed that no one came forward with information.

By nine o'clock that morning, the dorm room Courtney and Penny shared was thoroughly searched and all of Courtney's notebooks were removed. The school schedule went on as usual but a sense of dread filled each classroom. Teachers tried to keep the girls busy. Penny did her best to concentrate on her lessons but her thoughts kept drifting between pleas to God to take care of Courtney and guilt that she should have been more honest about the basement incident. Maybe if Courtney had been caught that night, this situation would have been averted.

Penny gathered her books and went to her math teacher's desk.

"Mrs. Richards, may I please be excused? I need to go see Mrs. Gibson." Tears welled in her eyes.

Mrs. Richards quickly wrote a hall pass and gave it to Penny.

"Do you need someone to go with you?" the teacher asked softly.

"No, madam," Penny responded. "I just need to talk to Mrs. Gibson about something I remember about Courtney."

"Then go on. Class is almost over. I'll see you tomorrow."

Penny walked across the quad to Bryant Hall and entered the door of the dining room. Not seeing Mrs. Gibson there, she headed toward the dorm mother's quarters. As she came down the hall, she heard voices she recognized coming from the lobby just around the corner.

"Baron, why would you volunteer for such as thing?"

"You heard the agent. They can't risk the Senator making the drop and they need someone of similar build and coloring. Like he said, it's uncanny how much I resemble him."

Penny interrupted their conversation.

"Resemble who?"

Baron looked at the young girl he loved more than anything in the world and knew he had to be honest with her.

"Penny, it seems I resemble Senator Guilford enough that I can make the ransom drop for him."

"No, Uncle Bear! It's too dangerous!" Penny shouted, bursting into tears.

Mrs. Gibson grabbed Penny and pulled her tear filled face into her shoulder. She looked at Baron with pleading eyes.

Baron sighed. He couldn't stand to see Penny so distraught.

"Penny, the agents say I'll be fine. All I have to do is drop the briefcase at the spot the kidnappers say. They are going to call at 1 o'clock. Please don't be afraid. The agents will be watching me and God will be with me. In His hands, I can't be any safer!"

Penny turned toward her uncle and wrapped her arms around his neck. She heard his words but, at that moment, nothing made sense. As Penny continued to sob, Rebecca guided her and Baron toward her nearby room. Coaxing Penny onto the bed and pulling a blanket over her, Mrs. Gibson sat beside the young girl until she fell asleep. Then she joined Baron who was sitting on a nearby couch.

"Baron, she can't take much more. She has been on such a roller coaster with Courtney for the last month. Then the kidnapping and now you getting involved in the case. She is sixteen but is still a fragile little girl in many ways."

"I know. But if I can help bring this case to a close, I have to do it. Please understand and help her to understand. I will be safe, I promise."

Baron put his arm around Rebecca and she laid her head on his shoulder. The two sat there watching the young girl they both loved so dearly. With God's grace, this storm would be over by the end of the day and all would be safe and well.

17

> "Have no fear of sudden disaster or of the ruin that
> overtakes the wicked, for the Lord will be your confidence
> and will keep your foot from being snared."
> Proverbs 3:25-26

Rebecca Gibson called the dean's office and filled Dean Merrick in on what was happening and that she would be staying in her room with Penny while Baron went with the FBI agents. She let Penny sleep while she and Baron prayed for the upcoming mission to find and rescue Courtney. They called the church and talked to the pastor. Getting assurance that a discreet prayer chain would be in place for the rest of the day, Baron kissed his sleeping niece and left her in the hands of her surrogate mother.

Baron Sanford went to his room and, per the agent's request, put on a suit and tie. He then went to the dean's office where he joined the agents, driving with them to the Guilford home. Baron walked into the home among a group of agents.

Once inside, Baron was introduced to Senator Martin Guilford who had been flown back to Charlotte from Washington by an army helicopter that morning.

"Senator, you know we can't let you make the drop. As a United States Senator, it would be too risky. Mr. Sanford, here, is willing to go in your place. Dressed in one of your suits and hats, we believe he will easily pass for you."

"Are you an agent, Mr. Sanford?"

"No, Sir, I work at Charlotte Hills Academy. Your daughter and my niece are roommates. I am quite willing to do whatever I can to help bring this to a happy ending."

"Well, thank you, Mr. Sanford. I am most grateful for your service. We all want a happy ending."

"I'm praying for that, Sir. So is Penny. May I ask how Mrs. Guilford is?"

"She's upstairs under sedation. A doctor is with her. If we don't get Courtney back soon…" The senator stifled back tears.

The senator called for one of his aides to take Baron upstairs to dress in the senator's clothes. Agent Copeland nodded at one of the other agents who followed them. The $50,000 demanded by the kidnappers was put in a briefcase. All was done and ready. Then the waiting began.

The telephone rang just as the grandfather clock in the Guilford den struck one. Martin Guilford answered the phone.

"Hello. Yes, I know where that is. First, I want to speak to Courtney. Please - wait. No! Stop, ok, I'll be there. No, no agents."

"She's alive. I heard her crying in the background. They must have been doing something to make her cry out," Martin reported as he sank into a chair. "They want the drop to be at the south end of the covered bridge in Central Park at 2 p.m."

"We need to get started. Which of your vehicles are you accustomed to driving yourself, Senator?"

"The Lincoln Continental. I'll have it brought to the front." He picked up the phone and gave instructions to someone in the garage. Hanging up, he addressed Baron one more time.

"My daughter is in your hands, Mr. Sanford. Please, bring her back to us. She is all we have. Here, take this hat. My hair has more gray than yours. We don't know how well they know what I look like."

"I'll do everything I can, Sir." Baron answered, nodding at the senator, and walking out the front door.

#####

Baron slipped into the leather seat of the Lincoln and turned the key in the engine. He carefully maneuvered the oversized car out the driveway of the Guilford estate and turned south toward Charlotte. He glanced at the Rolex that had been put on his arm by the agents and saw the time of 1:14. Baron chuckled at the thought of wearing a Rolex watch. His Timex had been a faithful companion for years and would be so jealous!

Another look at the watch showed 1:23. Just enough time to get to Central Park and walk to the bridge. The agents had been very specific about his tasks. He was to park, go to the bridge, leave the briefcase, and return to the car and drive back to the Guilford's. Nothing else. Baron had never thought of himself as the adventurous type and he had no desire to do more than make the drop.

1:52. Baron entered Central Park and pulled into a space as close to the covered bridge as possible. He got out of the car and stepped quickly toward the bridge. As he stepped off the path to place the briefcase underneath a bush, a man in a trench coat stepped in front of him.

"Good afternoon, Senator. Hold on to that briefcase and turn around. Walk back to the car. I have a gun in my pocket and will use it if you make any sudden moves or call attention to us. If I do use it, I will take the briefcase and your daughter!"

Baron caught his breath. He was no longer just a courier. He was now a kidnap victim! The two went to the car where Baron was told get in the driver's seat and drive. The kidnapper got in the passenger seat and held the gun on Baron as he dictated directions. West on 29 then south on 521. Four miles then turn right on dirt road where an old car is abandoned in the ditch. Once on the dirt road, the large car scrapped through overgrown brush for a half a mile before entering a clearing and coming to a stop in front of a ramshackle cabin.

"Get out of the car, Senator."

Baron slowly got out of the car and was escorted toward the cabin door.

"Open it," the man said.

Baron complied. There were no lights inside and the windows were boarded up. Baron rubbed his eyes to get used to the contrast of bright sunlight and darkness. He saw the figure of a blond girl on a cot in the corner. She was blindfolded.

A voice different from the one in the car spoke next.

"You got him! You actually got the Senator!"

"Daddy!" the girl screamed. "Daddy, is that you?"

"Go on, Senator. She's been waiting for you."

Baron rushed to the girl and embraced her as the men expected he would do. As he did he whispered in her ear that he was Penny's uncle as a decoy for her father.

"Play along. Someone is coming to help us," Baron said with all the hope and faith he could muster.

Baron and Courtney sat on the cot and held each other.

"Can I take the blindfold off her, please?" Baron asked.

The two kidnappers shrugged at each other.

"Suppose it won't do no harm. Neither one of you are going to live through this anyway," responded the older man.

Courtney cried out hysterically and Baron did what he could to comfort her. He pulled the blindfold off her eyes and held her close while she sobbed.

While the two kidnappers were counting the money in the briefcase, Baron held and rocked Courtney. After a few moments, she started to calm down and looked in the face of her comforter.

"Thank you for being here," she whispered. "Where are my parents?"

"They are safe. The FBI wouldn't let your father deliver the ransom. Probably for fear of this happening. Do you know these men, Courtney?"

"The one who stayed with me is Ken." Courtney took a deep breath. "I met him at my party. He said he liked me. We went out this weekend and he wanted to see me again so I agreed to meet him by the stables Sunday night. We walked through the woods to a road where he had a car and drove to this cabin. Ken gave me a drink that must have had something in it because when I woke up, both guys were here and I was blindfolded. They told me we were going to have a party and Daddy was going to pay the bill. They made a phone call and twisted my arm while they were on the phone."

Baron looked for the phone Courtney mentioned but it was on the other side of the room. Examining the bruises on Courtney's arm carefully, he got her to bend and rotate her arm to determine if it was broken.

"Looks like you have some bruises but I don't think anything is broken. Did they hurt you any other way?" he asked carefully.

"No. If either one had tried anything, well, I'll just say I would have given them the fight of their lives."

"I'm so sorry all this happened, Courtney. They have the ransom but must have something else in mind to grab me, too. God knows where we are and will help us. Will you believe that with me?"

"Believe in God? I've never believed in God. If there is a God, why would he let this happen?"

"Courtney, there are people who think that they can live by

their own rules. God has nothing to do with these men. It is evil they do and evil they live by."

"You said God knows where we are."

"He not only knows where we are, he is here, too."

"God is here?"

"Yes, Courtney. God said He would never leave me or forsake me. He is here with me because I am a child of His. He is my father."

Courtney smiled. "So God is going to take care of you? Do you think he'll include me in that favor?"

Baron hugged Courtney and patted her head, grateful that she had calmed to the point of conversing and smiling.

The two men were drinking beers and smoking at a table in the middle of the room. They had divided the money into two piles and were laughing about how they were going to spend $25,000 each.

"I'm going to quit that valet job and take a road trip," said the older man. "Let somebody else park my car for a change!"

"You're lucky," said Ken. "I'm still in high school. I'll have to hide my share for a while. It would be kind of suspicious for somebody my age to suddenly have cash!"

"Kid, this is just a drop in the bucket. If we got $50,000 for the daughter, I'm thinking we can get a half million for the Senator. It's a rich family. The wife is a Carpenter and can pay it from her personal fortune."

"Yea, she will. Courtney told me her mother really likes being a senator's wife. She'll do anything, pay anything to hold on to that kind of power."

"Too bad she has to lose the money and the power. No way we can give the girl or her dad back!"

Ken looked over at Courtney. He had liked her but when he told his cousin about her, Jim hatched this plan to get some money. He went along with it but thought it was just about money and nobody would get hurt. Now Jim was talking murder of both Courtney and her father!

Jim stood up and spoke in a hushed voice. "This is what we're going to do. We'll make another call and tell them to put a half million in a suitcase the wife will take to the bus station. She will sit in the waiting room and I will sit beside her and hand her a newspaper as a signal that I will be taking the suitcase. I'll just pick it up and walk out. What could be less conspicuous?"

"Man, there will be FBI all over that place!"

"Nah! We've got it made in the shade!"

Suddenly the door to the cabin burst open and Agent Copeland rushed in with four other agents, overtaking the surprised kidnappers. While Baron and Courtney were helped to their feet, Agent Copeland went to Baron and pulled an electronic device from the inside pocket of the suit coat Baron was wearing.

"You heard everything?" Baron exclaimed.

"Everything, Mr. Sanford. We had you bugged as soon as you put on the Senator's suit. They're not too smart. A couple of punks who live by their own rules!"

Their own rules! Baron smiled. They did hear everything. Not only did God know where they were but the FBI did, too!

Ken, handcuffed and standing against the wall, heard what the agent said.

"You're not Senator Guilford? Man, this thing is all messed up!"

Agent Copeland escorted Baron and Courtney out to a waiting car. Baron asked that the school be contacted and his niece informed of his safety. By the time they got back to the Guilford estate, Penny and Rebecca had been brought there by an agent. While Courtney was reunited with her parents, Baron rejoiced with Penny and Rebecca about his deliverance.

"Baron, I told you it was dangerous!" Rebecca chided.

"Rebecca, it's over now. I'm safe and Courtney is returned. It could have been bad but it wasn't. I trusted God the whole time. I even got Courtney to acknowledge that we were in God's hands."

Penny didn't say much. She had not been so frightened since the tornado had taken everything and everyone she loved except Uncle Bear.

"Penny, are you all right? I'm sorry you were scared. But God brought us through this storm and we will now see the rainbow of promise."

Penny again hugged her uncle's neck. Just then, Senator Guilford came to the den and invited the three to join him in the living room.

As soon as they saw each other, Penny and Courtney embraced. Courtney grabbed Penny's hand and asked her to go to her room and talk.

When the girls left, Rebecca sat with Mrs. Guilford and chatted. Senator Guilford took Baron aside and offered him a drink.

"No thank you, sir. I stopped drinking a long time ago when God allowed me to survive a very bad time."

"You've been through hard times?"

"Yes. But God is good and has given me a job I love, my niece to take care of, and so much to live for."

"While you were gone, I did some checking on you. You have a fine reputation at Charlotte Hills. I need someone like you on my staff. Are you interested?"

The sudden job offer intrigued Baron. Could this be the rainbow at the end of the storm?

"What kind of job, sir?"

"I have a fairly large staff here. A mechanic, chauffer, housekeeper, butler, two cooks, gardener, and a maintenance man. Taylor, the butler, has been overseeing everything but he is getting a bit senile. He'll do fine as a butler around the house but I need someone who will keep everything here at the estate running smoothly. I think you are the man for the job. It comes with a salary of $10,000 plus the use of a gatehouse that can accommodate a small family. How about it?"

Baron was stunned. $10,000 was three times what he currently made. And a house! He had seen the gatehouse as he entered the estate. It was a stone cottage that mimicked the big house. He finally would have a home for Penny and himself. And Rebecca! He could offer her a home as well!

Baron looked into the face of Martin Guilford and saw the sincerity of a man who was grateful to have his daughter back. He would seriously consider the offer.

"Thank you, sir for the generous offer. I am interested and will pray about it and talk with Penny. Now, if you will excuse us, our church is in revival and we want to go and thank God for all He did today."

"Revival, eh? I remember revival meetings from when I was a boy. Where is this one?"

Baron gave the Senator information about the church and the two men shook hands. Mrs. Guilford called Courtney and the girls came downstairs, laughing and talking like old friends. After saying their goodbyes, Baron, Rebecca, and Penny were driven back to Charlotte Hills by the Guilford chauffer. Baron looked at his two companions and quietly reflected on all God was continuing to do to fulfill his hopes and dreams.

18

The supper hour had passed when Penny got back to campus. Several girls had committed to go to revival services that evening, so there was only time to change clothes before leaving for the church. An announcement had been made at supper that Courtney had been found safe and well and all the girls were quite excited to find out the details from Penny who they had been told had gone to the Guilford home with Mrs. Gibson.

There were so many girls at the front of Bryant Hall to go to church that Baron got permission to take the bus. The girls were disappointed when Penny rode with Mrs. Gibson who was going to stop and get Penny something quick to eat since she hadn't had anything all day. The girls were miffed that they were left with just Penny's uncle, a man who was the school janitor. They would find out later they were actually being driven by a pivotal character in the drama that had unfolded that day.

Arriving at the church, the girls filed into the church and chatted fiercely about the day's events. When Penny arrived, they rushed her with questions but she just smiled and said they would talk later. The girls finally settled into several of the pews at the front of the church. Some of them had been there before, but for a few of the girls church was a new experience. All quieted down as the pastor and evangelist entered the sanctuary, showing great pleasure in seeing several rows of young women in the audience that night.

An exciting song service opened the revival meeting. The church building was comfortably full and all attention was toward the platform. No one noticed a family of three enter and squeeze into the back row.

At the conclusion of the song service, the pastor introduced the speaker.

"For those of you who may be part of these services for the

first time, I want to introduce you to a man who grew up denying that God existed. He found his pleasures in the world of power and prestige. At the age of 38, he owned three banks, and held interest in several large corporations you would recognize if I told you the names. His worldly interests included alcohol and gambling, the two addictions that brought his downfall. When he finally came to himself, like the prodigal son, he examined his life and found it diminished to nothing. He lost all his money, power, and friends. But unlike the prodigal son, he could not go home to his father, because all his life he had denied the existence of the God who made him, loved him, and died to save him for the consequence of sin. But then, like Saul on the road to Damascus, John Pierce met God and was born again. He comes tonight to share with us how God changed his life and called him to preach and minister to both the haves and have knots of this world, to show how, no matter what you are living for now, nothing is as important as knowing Jesus Christ as your Savior and Lord. Please welcome with me, our speaker, John Pierce!"

A rousing applause greeted the man who jumped onto the platform and for the next thirty-five minutes, captivated the audience with his testimony of life before and after his conversion. His description of how he had denied the existence of God was humorous. The contrast of his extensive financial fortune and the succession of events that left him broke and homeless left the audience stunned. But the strongest impression was made when John Pierce described his conversion experience and what God had restored to him in the ten years since he gave his life to God by accepting Jesus Christ as His Savior and Lord.

At the invitation at the end of the service, the aisle was filled with people responding to the call to surrender their lives to God. Several of the girls from Charlotte Hills Academy were in the group. Each one was talked with individually by the counselors that included Rebecca Gibson and Baron Sanford. Penny gathered the rest of the girls together and kept them occupied with cookies and Kool-Aid in the church social hall. They wanted to hear about Courtney but Penny put them off, telling them it was Courtney's story to tell.

Baron found Penny and corralled the girls toward the bus.

Penny rode home with the girls, happy about the outcome of the day's event and the response of her friends to the gospel message presented at the service.

Once back on campus, Penny hugged her uncle goodnight and hurried to Bryant Hall, eager to get her room back in order after the FBI search. As she worked, Penny hoped that the events of the last twenty-four hours would make a big difference in Courtney's attitude, behavior, and their relationship. Finally, she knelt at her bed and thanked God for his goodness and grace and protection of Courtney and Uncle Bear.

#####

Baron parked the bus and walked to Bryant Hall. Just as he knocked on Rebecca's door, she came down the stairs from the upstairs dorm rooms.

"Baron, what are you doing here? It's been such a long day, I thought you would have been eager to turn in as soon as you got the girls back."

Baron looked at Rebecca with a sudden clear understanding of his feelings about her. He loved her and was ready to risk expressing that love.

"Rebecca, can we talk?"

"Of course, Baron. Let's sit right here. I just rang lights out and all the girls should be in bed."

Rebecca sank into the lobby couch and Baron sat erect beside her, his arms hugging his knees and his head bowed.

"Baron, something is bothering you. What is the matter?"

Baron sighed deeply and leaned his head back onto the couch cushion, moving his clasped hands into his lap. He looked at Rebecca who was watching him with concerned eyes.

"Are you happy here, Rebecca?"

"Of course I am. Are you happy here? Are you thinking of leaving Charlotte Hills?"

"I was offered a job by Senator Guilford. It's an excellent position with salary and benefits that I would be foolish to turn down."

"Really? I know you, Baron. You would not take a job for the money. It would have to be in God's will and be good for Penny. Does this job meet that criteria?"

"Yes, but that's not the only criteria. It would have to be good for you, too, Rebecca. I love you and want you in my life. I want to ask you to be my wife. This isn't a proposal but notice that I want to give you a proposal. So a decision I make about this job has to include you."

Rebecca caught her breath and her eyes filled with tears. Words of intimacy between her and Baron had been unspoken for so long but the anticipation had been growing to a crescendo. Baron was everything she wanted in a husband—godly, kind, gentle, caring, and hard working. They had come from different worlds but the world that included Baron, Penny, and her is where she wanted to be the rest of her life.

Her eyes glistening, Rebecca blinked away her tears.

"Oh, Baron! I love you, too! I trust whatever God is leading you to do with your life. Whenever that proposal is made, I will be ready. Until then, I support you."

Baron reached over and took Rebecca's left hand in his. Stroking her fingers, he imagined putting a ring on that hand. He put his right arm around her shoulders and pulled her toward him. She said she loved him, too! How blessed he was! For a few moments, the beating of two hearts in sync with one another was the only sound in the quiet of the night.

At the ten o'clock chime of the clock, the two strolled to Rebecca's door and, for the first time, Baron embraced and kissed her.

"I thank God for you and the joy you have brought to my life," Baron whispered in Rebecca's ear before grabbing her hands and bowing his head in prayer. "Lord, we love you and trust you to work everything out for our good. Please continue to guide us in your will and your love. Amen."

"Amen," added Rebecca as she slipped through her door to have her own time of conversation with the Lord about all that had come to pass.

19

"Surely this is our God; we trusted in him, and he saved us. This is the Lord, we trusted in him; let us rejoice and be glad in his salvation." Isaiah 25:9

Breakfast on Wednesday was abuzz with excitement about Courtney who returned to campus Tuesday evening while Penny and many of the girls were gone to the revival service. When she came into the dining room, Courtney was flooded with girls who wanted to hear about what had happened. She complied with a very dramatic description of the kidnapping. The way she talked, strangers grabbed her and kept her hostage for a lot of money. She didn't tell the part about going to meet Ken willingly and that the boyfriend she had bragged about last week was the one who held her hostage.

Courtney included in her narration the role Penny's uncle had played in her rescue. The girls were surprised at the news and wondered why Penny had not told them. Penny just smiled when asked about her uncle and acknowledged that her uncle was very brave and wonderful!

Courtney's treatment of Penny was quite different than it had been during previous weeks. When Penny got back from revival on Tuesday night, Courtney was there with gifts that included a bouquet of flowers on Penny's desk and new bedding on her bed.

After welcoming her roommate with an embrace, Penny immediately noticed the new spread on her bed.

"Where's my quilt?" Penny asked in a panicked voice.

"I put that old thing in your closet. It was so worn and tattered. Wanted you to have a nice, new one."

Penny looked at Courtney. She meant well. But Courtney did not know how much that old quilt meant to her. Maybe it was time Penny opened up and trusted Courtney with her story.

With tears in her eyes, Penny retrieved her quilt and sat on her bed, stroking the quilt against her face.

"Penny, why are you crying? Don't you like your new bed set?"

"It's very nice but, well, Courtney, come sit with me. Let's talk."

"Sure, Penny. Hey, it was so much fun having you at my house. Glad you got to see my bedroom."

"It was nice to visit your home. The circumstances were terrible but I think what happened will help us be better friends. You want us to be friends, don't you?"

"Of course! What your uncle did for me cinched everything. He was my hero! I'm sorry for all the mean things I've said about him and you. Will you forgive me?"

Penny looked at Courtney with amazement. What a difference a few days had made in this girl!

"I forgive you, Courtney. You didn't know me or my uncle. But I'd like to tell you about where we came from. Would you like to hear our story?"

"Oh, yes!"

The two girls sat on the bed and Penny opened up her hurtful past more than she had ever done before.

"I was born in a little town in western North Carolina. My grandparents lived down the road and so did my aunt Helen and Uncle Bear. His real name is Baron but I started calling him Bear when I learned to talk and never stopped. Everybody I knew were farmers and we didn't have much money. I guess you could say we were poor, very, very poor.

"When I was five years old, my parents joined the carnival. Because they were gone for months at a time, I was living with Aunt Helen and Uncle Bear. They didn't have children and I pretended I was their little girl. I loved them so much. Aunt Helen took good care of me, helped me start school and took me to church. Uncle Bear took care of both of us. We were very happy."

Penny stopped her narration and picked up the quilt from her lap, tenderly fingering the fabric.

"Aunt Helen liked to sew and she made my clothes. She used the material from my old clothes and made this quilt for me. I've been sleeping with it for as long as I can remember."

Taking a deep breath, Penny prepared herself for the next part of the story. She looked at Courtney who was gently grasping the edge of the quilt as if trying to touch the past Penny was describing.

"What happened to your family, Penny?" Courtney asked softly.

"My parents returned from a carnival trip to Florida and the whole family was getting ready to celebrate Easter together. Aunt Helen and I gathered eggs from the henhouse, cooked them, and colored them for a town egg hunt on Saturday. But that Friday night was stormy and we wondered if the party would be rained out. It was worse than that. A tornado hit our town and forty seven people died."

"Oh, no," Courtney exclaimed, her hand going to her mouth. "Your family, Penny? Did they die, too?"

"I was asleep when Uncle Bear picked me and my quilt, this quilt, up and carried me to the storm shelter. Aunt Helen was right behind us but didn't make it in time. My parents and grandparents were killed, too. Courtney, that's why this quilt is so special to me. It's the only thing I have that survived the storm. When Uncle Bear and I came out of the shelter, everything and everybody was gone."

Tears were falling down Courtney's face. Penny reached over and grabbed her roommate's hand.

"It was a long time ago, Courtney. I was seven years old and since then, God has given me so much to replace what was lost. I know I will see Aunt Helen again in heaven. I hope I see my parents and grandparents but I don't think so. They didn't give any evidence of knowing God and believing in Jesus as their Savior."

"That's what the preacher said at your church isn't it? Jesus died for our sins and we have to believe in Him to have God's salvation."

Penny looked at Courtney in surprise.

"You were at my church? When?"

"Your uncle told my dad about the meeting. Daddy, Mom, and I were there Monday night after we finished talking to the FBI agents. We met with the speaker after the service. Penny, I don't know what happened but Daddy and Mom have both changed."

"And you, Courtney? Have you changed?"

"I certainly have thought about things different. Your uncle told me that God was with us in that cabin. He told me to trust God to help us. Penny, your uncle was never afraid! He really believed what he was saying. It was right after that the agents came in and rescued us!" Courtney declared, smiling broadly.

"So is God still dead?" Penny grinned.

"He wasn't Monday night! And I think I met him at the church. When the speaker asked us to invite Jesus to come into our heart, I did. When we talked to the speaker after church, he said that if we prayed those words and believed that Jesus would do it, we were saved. I don't know what saved means but I did mean that prayer."

"Oh, Courtney! I am so happy to hear that! Being saved means that you will never face the consequences of your sins because Jesus died for them. Not that it's o.k. to sin but if you do and confess, God is faithful to forgive you and clean you from all your sin."

"Is that what you do when you pray in the morning, confess your sins?"

"Well, I pray that prayer before I go to sleep every night. In the morning, I talk to God about my problems and ask his help and guidance in decisions I have to make. Praying is like having a heart to heart with your best friend."

"Can I join you in the morning? I want to learn how to pray."

"Nothing would make me happier, Courtney! Let's start right now." Penny slipped off her bed and knelt down. Courtney followed suit. Penny began to pray.

"Dear Lord, thank you for all you have done for me today. Thank you for my friend Courtney who has asked you to come into her heart. Help me to be the example to her of a believer and help her know you and your Word. Forgive me of my sins, those things that I have done that have not been pleasing to you. Forgive me, too, for what I have not done for you that I should. I love you, Lord and ask all this in Jesus name, Amen."

When Penny finished, she started to get up but a hand on her arm stopped her.

"Dear Lord, thank you for all you have done for me today. Thank you for coming into my heart and giving me a roommate like Penny who will teach me to pray. Forgive me of my sins. Forgive me for taking Penny's quilt. In Jesus' name, Amen."

Just then the lights out bell rang.

"Mrs. Gibson is on the job," Courtney said. "That reminds me." Courtney bowed her head again. "God, forgive me for telling lies about Mrs. Gibson. Amen."

Raising her head, she smiled at a started Penny.

"I started those rumors about Mrs. Gibson. I'll ask her to forgive me tomorrow. We better get to bed. Penny, I'm sorry I took your quilt. Will you forgive me?"

"Oh, yes! If God has forgiven you, I have to, too! And I have no doubt Mrs. Gibson will forgive you."

The girls got up and hugged each other, then turned off the lights and went to bed. Penny lay in her bed and silently praised God for what He had done in Courtney's life. She told the Lord she would do her part to disciple her and help her to grow in His grace. The storm named Courtney was over and Penny could sleep in peace.

20

> "The salvation of the righteous comes from the Lord;
> he is their stronghold in time of trouble.
> The Lord helps them and delivers them;
> he delivers them from the wicked and saves them,
> because they take refuge in him."
> Psalm 37:39-40

The revival services ended on Friday night with a large crowd coming together for a praise service. The Guilford family was in attendance. After several testimonies, the pastor told the congregation the senator had requested the opportunity to address the congregation. An accomplished speaker, Senator Guilford seemed at a loss for words at first but then, in simple eloquence, told the events of the past Sunday and Monday. He thanked those who had prayed for the situation. He publicly thanked Baron Sanford for his role in the recovery of his daughter and for the invitation to the services that his family had accepted. He then surprised those present with his confession.

"I have accomplished much in this life. I have money, power, and status. But I have learned this week through the simple faith and courage of Baron Sanford and the preaching of John Pierce that I really have nothing of eternal significance. I had never acknowledged God and certainly had no regard for the Bible or anything spiritual. What I came to realize I am in desperately in need of salvation. After Monday's service, I spoke with Rev. Pierce and was shown God's simple plan to save me from my sins. Just like I was willing to pay a ransom for my daughter, I learned Jesus had paid the ransom for my soul. I asked Jesus to come into my heart and he did."

A rousing applause welcomed that announcement. The senator held up his hand to the crowd.

"I want to add my testimony to this praise service. I thank God for all He has brought me and my family through this week and using this time and these circumstances as an instrument to show me my need of his salvation. I thank God for keeping my daughter safe from harm. I thank God for men like Baron Sanford who are willing to give their lives to save others. And finally, I thank God for everyone in this church who has shown me what a community of faith is supposed to be. God bless each and every one of you."

Another round of applause followed Senator Guilford as he left the pulpit and moved toward his family, accepting the handshakes of many between the platform and the pew. After the senator spoke, the pastor once again introduced John Pierce.

The sermon that night was about the steps of growing in faith. The evangelist challenged each mature Christian to take on a new believer to disciple. Penny found an empty space in her Bible and wrote the sermon outline she could use later with Courtney. For the last few mornings, Courtney had gotten up with Penny and the two had devotions together. Courtney had even invited other girls to join them. That Friday morning, five girls were in Penny's room, each with a Bible in their hands provided by Mrs. Gibson and listening as Penny read scripture and led them in a prayer meeting.

At the end of the service, the three Guilford's walked down the aisle and made their professions of faith. Several others did as well, ending the revival with an excitement that thrilled the congregation. Baron Sanford drove the few students who were returning to Charlotte Hills back to the campus and then he and Penny left campus again for a late date at an ice cream shop. Baron wanted to talk to Penny about their future.

Sitting in a booth with banana splits in front of them, Baron opened up to his niece.

"Penny, we've had quite an exciting week, haven't we?"

"It's been a wonderful week, Uncle Bear. You and Courtney are both safe and Courtney and her parents are now Christians. I don't think it could get any better!"

"Perhaps it could. Senator Guilford has offered me a job on his staff. The benefits include a house and a very good salary. You can stay at Charlotte Hills as a regular student. What do you think?"

The news was a surprise to Penny. It certainly would be a change for the two of them. To be in a real house was a dream come true. She would come and go to Charlotte Hills like most of the girls, spending her weekends away from the campus.

"Oh, Uncle Bear! Is it a job you would like to have?"

"Yes. I have prayed for a long time for a job that would provide us a home where we could be together. And it would also allow something else."

"What is that?"

"Penny, I love Rebecca. I want to ask her to marry me. Would you approve of that?"

"Would I approve? Oh, Uncle Bear, I think that is the most wonderful news of all! Will she say yes?"

Baron grinned. "I believe she will. I wanted to speak to you first. I am meeting with Senator Guilford tomorrow to accept his offer and find out when I will begin the job. I will give my notice to the academy on Monday. As soon as all of these formalities are confirmed, I will propose to Rebecca. She will be a wonderful mother for you."

"Yes she will but no more wonderful that you have always been, Uncle Bear. I love you so much."

"I've loved being your Uncle Bear, Penny. I would love being your father. What do you think? Could you call me father?"

Penny got up and put her arms around his neck and planted a kiss on each cheek. "No, I can't call you father but I would love to call you, Daddy."

EPILOG

Baron Sanford began his job as Guilford Properties Manager on November 1. On November 10, he and Rebecca Gibson were married in a simple but beautiful ceremony at their church. Rebecca retired from Charlotte Hills and began writing devotional materials for Youth for Christ. Penny and Courtney continued as roommates and sisters in the Lord, Courtney absorbing all that Penny taught her about her new Christian faith. Courtney joined the Grace Livingston Hill Reading Club and her mother funded the purchase of a complete set of books for the dorm. Each Friday afternoon after the club meeting, the girls rode back to the Guilford estate together where Rebecca greeted Penny with a hug, cookies, and milk.

Rebecca and Baron excitedly announced at the church Easter service their expectation of a child. On August 28, 1965 Baron Robert Sanford, Jr. was born to the delight of his parents and sister Penny who called him Baby Bear.

Sanctity Series

As a teenager and young adult, I was an avid reader of Grace Livingston Hill. Her stories of young people growing up with grace and purity showed me a value system that was worth emulating as I made my own choices.

God has given me several stories of my own that I am presenting through the **Sanctity Series,** stories of people who seek to live in and through God's grace. *Storm Chaser* is the second in this series. The first book, *Prescription for Truth* is available from the author, CreateSpace.com, or Amazon.com.

Coming titles in this series:

Quilt Pieces
For Sarah and Luke Landon, the juggling of marriage, careers, children, and the stresses of everyday life unravels what is supposed to be a perfect family. The search to find the pattern to make sense of their life takes many paths. Will they put the pieces back together before it is too late?

Evidence of Love
When her husband dies under puzzling circumstances, Abigail Waterston is thrown into a mystery that sends her on a search for truth, courage, and faith that will sustain as she moves on to the next chapter of her life.

This Side of Sunset (sequel to *Prescription for Truth)*
Ready to retire, Margaret Sutton anticipated relaxation, volunteer work, and time to love and enjoy family when a sudden health crisis threatens, taking her on a uncertain journey toward the sunset of her life.

Comments? Contact me:
Cheryl Weavers Stacey, clstacey@att.net, 850-455-9486

CPSIA information can be obtained
at www.ICGtesting.com
Printed in the USA
BVOW06s1926221116
468642BV00013B/179/P

9 781453 726211